THE SILENT BOY

A SLOANE MONROE MYSTERY

CHERYL BRADSHAW
JANET FIX

First US edition July 2021

eBook ISBN: 9798201814861
Paperback ISBN: 9798536508343

THE SILENT BOY

New York Times & USA Today
Bestselling Author

CHERYL BRADSHAW
& JANET FIX

"You can always lie to others and hide your actions from them... but you cannot fool yourself."

- Abraham Lincoln

1

In the dirty hallway of a local tavern, six-year-old Louie Alvarez played with his little race cars as he waited for his mother to take him home. He sometimes hung out there while she finished the early shift as a waitress. Today was one of those days. To keep himself occupied, he drove the cars along the rough planks of the floor and the patchy stucco of the walls, making whirring noises as they went up and down, round and round ...

A scream shook the air.

Startled, Louie shot up, one hand clutching a race car and the other grabbing his pants to keep from peeing himself. Heart pounding, he stared at the door at the end of the hallway. The scream had come from inside that room.

Who had screamed?

And why?

His *mom* was in that room.

In the past, Louie had overheard the men who frequented the tavern call it the Family Meeting Room, a name he considered silly. He'd watched them shuffle in and out, and at times a woman or two —like his mom—but no kids. Once, when no one was looking, he'd entered the room and looked around, disappointed when all he found was a large round table, a bunch of chairs, and little else. A weathered, dust-covered dresser rested in one corner. The table was littered with ashtrays, empty glasses, and bottles of alcohol, something his mother had warned was off limits to him at all times.

With his back against the wall, Louie shuffled toward the other end of the hallway. He inched closer and closer until he noticed the door was cracked open just a bit. He wanted to peek inside, to see what was going on, but how could he without getting caught?

Louie took a slow breath in and out, careful not to utter a sound. He was the best at sneaking around, better than all his friends—so good, in fact, it had often angered his mother. She hated when he creeped up on her. She'd hold a hand to her chest, shout a cuss word, and say, "You almost gave me a heart attack, Louie!" And then they'd both laugh because she could never stay mad at him for long.

Louie reached the door, but before he got his chance to peer inside, a second scream trumpeted through the stale air, followed by a loud bang, and lots of yelling. He swallowed away his fear, approached the crack in the door, and glanced inside. A short man with a big, round belly had the boy's mom backed up against the wall. She was crying, and her face was red, her nose bloody.

Louie didn't know who this man was. At least he couldn't remember ever having seen him before. The man wore a sleeveless black shirt, and running down the entire length of his arm, there was a tattoo of a massive snake curled around a big knife. He knew what a tattoo was because lots of people had them. One day he might get one too, except his wouldn't be as scary.

Eyes wide as frisbees, Louie watched the man slap his mom hard on the side of her head.

"We've had enough of you, Ginny!" the man yelled. "It's over. Done. We can't allow you—one stupid, big-mouthed woman—to bring the whole thing down. You must know that!"

The man grabbed Ginny by the hair and shoved her to the ground. Terror-stricken and shaking, Louie's mother continued to cry, begging them to stop. Louie wondered what she had done to anger the man ... and why he was hitting her.

Was there anything he could do to help?

Could he save her?

Someone crossed Louie's line of sight, someone other than the man hurting his mother. Louie jerked back and flattened himself against the wall. How many more people were in there?

A second voice echoed through the room. "You're making too much noise, you idiot. What the hell are you doing?"

The voice sounded familiar to Louie, but he wasn't sure when or where he'd heard it before. His mind was all confused.

The tattoo guy, the one who'd hit his mom, said, "Yeah, whatever. You take over, then."

Louie wrinkled his nose and snarled his lips but didn't move a muscle. He didn't even breathe. The last time he'd felt this way was the day his father died. Even now, the sadness and fear Louie had over his death lingered inside him.

For a moment, the room fell silent. Louie chanced another glance but couldn't see much more than his mother on the ground near the wall.

The familiar voice, low and menacing, said, "We are all in agreement, Ginny. This doesn't have to be complicated."

A gun was raised, pointed at his mom's head. Louie couldn't see the person holding it, but he knew one thing: guns were for shooting.

Who would want to shoot his mom?

She whimpered and begged for her life. She said she was sorry and promised to keep her mouth shut. The gun was lowered, and for a moment, Louie breathed a sigh of relief. The mean people would accept his mom's apology. They'd let her go now.

Everything would be all right.

He was sure of it.

The gun came back into view. “Such a beautiful face you have, Ginny. What a pity.”

A loud crack ripped through the air as Louie’s mom was shot in the center of her forehead.

Louie gasped and cried out, dropping his race car.

Chairs scraped along the floor inside the room. Hissing voices said, “Who was that?”

Louie heard the sound of footsteps rushing toward him. He tried to run and couldn’t. His legs were stiff and immovable. It was like they’d been superglued to the floor. For all his clever sneaking around in the past, this moment was a bad time to fail. Louie wished he’d never crept to the door in the first place. He wished he’d never looked inside.

But he had, and it was too late now.

They were coming for him.

2

"We're at the beach, baby," Maddie exclaimed. She bobbed her head, stuck her lips out like a duck, and snapped her fingers. "Ohhh yeahhh. Uh-huh. Oh yeah."

Maddie and I had just arrived within the city limits of Tarpon Springs, Florida, amidst the staggering heat that was summertime in these parts.

I turned toward her and rolled my eyes. "First, you look ridiculous doing that lip thing. Second, I see no beach. Third, it's hot as hell. Why must we have the windows open?"

She raised a brow and flashed me an even bigger set of duck lips. "Oh, come on. Relax. It's all part of the experience."

I fanned my armpits with some brochures I'd snagged at a gas station and held my arms up to the open window. At least I was dressed weather-appropriate in khaki shorts and a blue-and-white striped sleeveless blouse. Even if I didn't feel cool, I gave off the appearance of being cool. It wasn't ideal, but it was something.

I glanced over at Maddie and stifled a laugh. She was my best friend, and one of the most brilliant women I'd ever known, but at times she acted like she was still twenty-five. Or fifteen, depending on the day. Dressed in a glittery bronze bikini and unzipped cut-off denim shorts rolled down just enough to show off her cute pot belly, she'd taken the weather-appropriate dress code to a whole new level. The matching triangle bikini top twinkled in the sunshine coming through the windshield. She was like one big sparkle.

I snickered and said, "I love you, you know that?"

She chomped on the gum in her mouth and gave me a curious look. "Well, of course you do. I brought you to the beach!"

Known as "the sponge capital of the world" and chock-full of Greek tradition, Tarpon Springs was our first stop on the summer journey we'd agreed to months earlier. Maddie had insisted on the trip *and* making all the plans. It worried me. I wasn't used to being left out of the loop, and as far as I could tell, there was no *actual* plan. All she'd told me so far was that we were going to do the tourist thing, meet up with some of her family along the way, and eat a lot of Greek food. There was no set itinerary, no prearranged lodging, nothing—heck, we weren't even sure how long we'd be staying in the area. It was all *fly by the seat of our pants* stuff, Maddie's usual MO —craziness.

Now that I was in my late forties, married to Cade, and semi-retired from the private-investigator business I'd owned for the last fifteen years, I'd made a commitment to embrace my newfound freedom. And with all this freedom floating around me, waiting for me to take a bite, I had decided to ... well, bite.

Maddie, a retired medical examiner, had been adamant for us girls to "escape," as she'd called it. My commitment to myself was similar: hang out with her for a while, have some fun, travel, see the sights. Most of all, I planned to relax, something I'd never been good at. This trip was my chance to evolve, to become a new worry-free me. I'd even allowed my signature pixie cut to grow out and now wore it in a sharp bob with little strips of blond scattered throughout my dark hair. The style change had taken some convincing. Maddie had said it would make me look younger, and she was right; it did.

Or maybe I just *felt* younger. To sweeten the pot, Cade loved the new look too.

I leaned back in the seat and smiled. Ever since I'd moved back to California, I hadn't seen Maddie as much as I would have liked. In my mind, it was time for happy hour, every hour. Why not?

I turned toward Maddie and held up a finger.

"Mm-yesss?" she asked.

The sun's afternoon rays had found her blond hair and caused the long braid dangling over her shoulder to glisten like it had been sprayed with glitter.

"I know you want some of your plans to be a surprise," I said, "but can we at least pull over so we can figure out where we're staying tonight?"

She considered my request, and then jerked the wheel to the right. We came to an abrupt stop in the middle of a shopping center off US 19. I did a Google search, and we narrowed down our options. Her sister Ginny lived in the area, but we wanted a little more freedom than staying with family could sometimes afford. We settled on Lynn's Inn. It was quaint, and according to the bio in the inn's "About Us" section, the owner was well informed in all things Greek and Tarpon Springs. She'd lived in town all her life. She'd married a Greek boy. Had Greek babies. Cooked like only a Greek could. It seemed like the perfect choice.

The inn was situated on Tarpon Ave. downtown, just minutes away from the famous Spring Bayou, one of three bayous in the city. According to Maddie, it was the site of the Epiphany, where the archbishop of the Greek church threw a blessed cross into the water and a slew of young Greek boys dove in to retrieve it. Once a year, in early January, this sacred event still occurred. The youth who nabbed the cross received a year of blessings.

We pulled into the gravel parking lot at the side of the inn, and I was taken aback with the surroundings: lush greenery, massive cacti, a wide wraparound front porch, adorable garden accents … and a Victorian-style home with a crisp yellow exterior and red trim.

The inn's side door opened, and a woman with dark hair and a wide smile stepped out. She waved her hands in front of her and said, "Ladies, welcome to Lynn's Inn! I'm Lynn."

I smiled back and a single thought sprang to mind … *Show me the beach!*

3

We settled into our room upstairs, which was as charming in décor as the rest of the inn, and Lynn said goodbye, reminding us to stop by the kitchen later for a slice of homemade cherry pie.

I glanced at Maddie. "Where should we go first?"

"Hmm," she said. "Let's check out the docks."

Maddie was referring to the Sponge Docks and surrounding areas, where tourists came to mingle. And it was just a hop-skip-and-jump away from the inn. We headed down Dodecanese Blvd., the main drag for the docks, and did a preliminary run through the area. Big fishing boats were tied to moorings along the concrete seawall of the Anclote River, which fed into the local bayous and then the Gulf of Mexico. An impressive statue of a sponge diver along one of the walkways attested to the Greek heritage of the city. Many side streets branched from Dodecanese, and the entire place brimmed with clothing shops, candy shops, soap shops, dessert shops, wine shops, and restaurants—everything two women on vacation could want.

Over the next hour we popped into a handful of stores, and while it was relaxing at first, it wasn't long before I was all shopped out. When Maddie pointed out yet another aroma-loaded soap shop, I threw in the towel and said, "Go on ahead. I think I'll just meander through the area for a while. Call me when you're ready to eat, okay?"

She nodded. "If you see any sexy Greek men while you're *meandering,* feel free to point them in my direction. You might be taken. I'm not."

She tossed her head back, laughed at her own joke, and then stepped inside the soap shop. I headed down the sidewalk, turning in circles every now and then as I walked. The gulf waters, the fishing boats, the people from all over the world, the businesses ... It was low-key yet exciting at the same time.

I rounded a corner and heard someone sobbing in the distance. I spun around, trying to locate where the sound had come from. I looked left, then right, and then I saw him. A boy around six years old appeared to be running for his life. His face was streaked with tears, and his nose was snotty. His expression said it all—he was terrified.

I wondered why.

Several feet behind the boy, a wiry man with a goatee speed-walked in the boy's direction, his eyes fixed on him. As the boy drew closer to me, I held my hands out and stooped down a bit in an attempt to meet him at eye level when he passed. The man who seemed to be following the boy looked me in the eye and then backpedaled, disappearing down a narrow alleyway.

I shifted my attention back to the boy and said, "Hey, are you all right?"

He swished past like he hadn't seen me and kept on going.

I stared down at my flimsy sandals and sighed.

Okay, I'm not prepared for a marathon, kid.

I canvassed the area. No one else seemed to know the boy, and I wondered why the man following him took off when we made eye contact. And where were the boy's parents? He was far too young to be left on his own, and it was clear he was upset about something. I looked down at my sandals again, shrugged, and decided they'd have to do. I broke into a jog and shouted, "Hey, kid. I just want to make sure you're okay. Please. Stop for a second so I can talk to you."

He glanced over his shoulder at me and then picked up the pace.

Wonderful.

I pushed myself harder until I came within an arm's reach. Then I grabbed his shirt and spun him around. Out of breath, I managed a simple, "What's wrong?"

No response.

"What's wrong? Are you lost? Did you get separated from your mother?"

No response.

I kept pressing.

"What's your name?"

Nothing.

Maybe he wasn't talking because his parents had taught him not to talk to strangers. Still, with no parents in sight, I needed to know what was going on.

"Why are you crying? Do you know where your parents are?"

He shifted his focus to the ground and continued to give me the silent treatment. I contemplated what to do next. Did I just leave him and let him go on his way? It seemed like a cruel thing to do to a child with no adult around to supervise him.

Behind me, someone yelled my name. I whipped around and saw Maddie sprinting toward me. I stepped aside, my hand still on the boy's shoulder, so she could see him.

Maddie squinted at him and stopped short. "Louie?"

I looked at the boy and then at her. "Do you know him?"

"Yeah, he's Ginny's son, my nephew."

Whatever I'd expected her to say, it wasn't what she'd just said.

I filled her in on what had happened. When I finished, she bent down, took his hand in hers, and said, "Louie, this is my friend Sloane. You wanna tell Aunt Maddie what's going on?"

He shook his head, and his long brown curls fell around his face.

Maddie glanced up at me. "The last time I talked to my sister, she mentioned he's been having a hard time"—she frowned at Louie and lowered her voice—"since his dad, Diego, died a few months back. We haven't spoken a whole lot since then, just a few texts back and forth. I told you all about his dad dying, right?"

"You didn't, but at least we know where he belongs now," I said.

"If he won't talk to us, maybe he'll talk to his mother." Maddie pulled her cell phone out of her pocket and made a call. A moment later, she scrunched up her nose and said, "My sister's not picking up on her cell. I wonder why. It's not like her to leave Louie unattended like this. We should get him home. Maybe she's there."

The boy's dark-brown eyes widened, his long eyelashes still damp with tears. He furrowed his brow, shaking his head in a violent manner. It seemed he didn't want to go home, didn't want to see his mother, or maybe both.

Interesting.

I gave him a look that said: *Too bad, kid. I want some answers.* Then I elbowed Maddie. "I'm not sure what's happening with him, but I do know one thing—something doesn't feel right."

4

We arrived at Ginny's place, an impressive one-story Mediterranean-style home stretched across a lush, manicured lawn, and I approached the front door. I knocked. No one answered. I knocked again, a bit harsher this time. Still nothing. Hoping the door might be unlocked, I twisted the knob. It wasn't.

Enough of this. I'll break my way in if I have to, but first ...

I turned toward the car, where a sullen Louie still sat in the back seat, his arms crossed, lip quivering. Maddie was holding the door open, trying to coax him out. He wouldn't budge.

"Louie, sweetie, do you have a key to your mom's house?" I asked.

I was just about to check and see if there were any open windows when Louie slid out of the car. Maddie put an arm around him, gave him an encouraging squeeze, and they walked toward the porch. Louie looked at Maddie and then pointed to a huge potted palm.

"The key's there?" she asked.

He nodded and wiped his nose.

Since the pot was too heavy to lift, I knew it wasn't logical for the key to be hidden beneath it. I sifted around in the soil and discovered the key in a small box buried amongst the roots of the plant.

I unlocked the door and went in first, scanning the room for an alarm system. There was one, but it wasn't engaged. I ushered Maddie and Louie into the foyer and stood a moment, taking in the coziness of the beach décor. Lots of wood. Tans, blues, and whites. Massive cushions and plush area rugs.

"Ginny, you here?" Maddie shouted.

There was a bark and the jangle of a collar. Unsure of what type of dog Ginny had or its temperament, I put my arms out to protect Maddie and Louie if needed. It was ridiculous, of course. *I* was the stranger here. Seconds later, an adorable black and white Shih Tzu trotted into the living area. I heard two claps and turned to see Louie kneeling down, beckoning for the dog to come to him. The dog jumped into his arms, and Louie buried his face in the dog's fur.

"Awww, he's a cutie," I said. "What's his name?"

I hoped now that we were in his home, among familiar surroundings, he'd say something. He didn't. His face remained buried in the dog's fur.

I looked at Maddie. "Do you know the dog's name?"

"I didn't even know my sister had a dog. Last time we spoke, she didn't."

I wondered if Ginny had gotten the dog for Louie, to help ease the pain after losing his father.

Maddie called the tavern where Ginny worked. She wasn't there either. Unsure of what to do next, she crossed in front of me and entered the kitchen. "I'll make some coffee while we wait, I guess. Ginny should be home soon."

She then eyeballed Louie. "It would help if you would talk to us, mister. We'd sure like to know what's going on."

"I'm sure he will in time," I said. "It's okay. Right, Louie?"

He released the dog and shrugged.

I shrugged too.

Maddie shook her head and returned to the chore of making coffee. I took a seat at the table. The dog walked under it and nestled in next to my shoe. Louie leaned against the wall and began to cry.

My heart wrenched, and I reached out to him, surprised when he grabbed my hand and held it tight, his chubby fingers almost going white from the effort. I breathed in a deep sigh and said, "Listen, sweetie. Everything's going to be okay. Maybe your mom's busy right now. Is there a friend who sometimes takes care of you? A family member who lives here? Anyone we can call?"

Silence.

Face down.

Still holding my hand.

I pressed on. "Can you help us find your mom? Please?"

Silence.

Face down.

Still holding my hand.

"You wanna know what I think?" I said. "I think something scary happened to you today, and I understand you might be too frightened to talk about it. Why don't we try a different way to talk to each other, something that doesn't involve words? Does that sound better?"

He looked up and gave me a slight nod.

I smiled.

It was something.

Maddie cleared her throat, and I turned to see an old-fashioned address book dangling from her hand. She opened it to the front page, set it on the counter, and then waggled a finger at Louie. "Come over here for a minute, please."

He and I both approached, and she pointed at the page.

I looked to where she had pointed and read: *Contacts for Louie*. I couldn't believe our luck. Beneath the headline were the words: *In case of emergency call ...*

And there it was, inked in black pen.

We had a name.

5

While Maddie called Tara Simmons, the first person listed as Louie's emergency contact in the address book, I spent some time working with Louie in hopes of getting him to open up. Since he didn't seem ready to talk, I stuck to things he could show me, if possible.

"What's your favorite food?" I asked.

He opened the cupboard and pointed to a mac-n-cheese in a box.

"I used to eat mac-n-cheese when I was your age too. What's your dog's name?"

It turned out to be a winning question, because he led me to the laundry room, where there was a dog bed, leashes, and a bowl with the name CHARLIE written on it.

Not long after Maddie's call with Tara had ended, Tara arrived at the house, blazing through the front door and into the kitchen. She looked to be in her early forties and had long, straight red hair and an abundance of freckles on her makeup-free face. She wore a white peasant blouse tucked into a denim skirt and a pair of worn, brown Birkenstocks, which revealed a ring on one of her toes. A slew of bangles covered her wrists, and her necklaces swayed with every step, along with a pair of heavy, multi-tiered earrings. It all looked like costume jewelry—nothing ritzy—but there was a lot of it, except for her fingers, which were bare.

Tara pounced on Louie, showering him with hugs and kisses. "Oh, sweet boy. You okay, love?"

He just sat there, unmoving.

So odd.

Maddie got us all settled with some coffee—milk for Louie—and a pack of Oreos to share. Introductions were made, and I learned that Tara was a close friend of the family and often took care of the boy when his mother worked. Tara was looking for a job, had no kids of her own, and was married to a man named Nick, who worked for a drywall company. "Exhausting, messy work" was how she described it. But they did whatever it took to make ends meet. She considered Louie to be like the son she would never be able to have —her husband was sterile. Though the last tidbit was a little TMI, I was sympathetic to her plight and grateful to have someone around who knew Louie so well.

I redirected the small talk to some serious talk. "Any idea where we might find Louie's mother?"

Tara seemed to be taken aback by my abrupt approach, but we'd dallied enough.

She shrugged and said, "I'm not sure. I know she had to work this morning. I gave the tavern a call on my way here. No one knows where she's at."

"Let's go to her work and talk to the employees who worked with her today. And in the meantime, how about you try calling Ginny's cell phone? Maybe she'll pick up for you."

I gestured toward the phone she'd placed on the table when she arrived.

"I tried calling several times already," Tara said. "No answer." She bit down on her lip. "There's something you should know about ..."

She threw an obvious side-eye at Louie.

Whatever she needed to say, it seemed like she didn't want to do it in front of him.

I stood and reached for his hand. "Adults need to talk now, but we won't take long. I promise. You okay to go to your room for a few minutes?"

Louie nodded, and we walked to his bedroom. Charlie scampered along behind us, which made me feel better about leaving him alone while we talked. At least Louie would have a furry companion with him. Letting go of his hand, I leaned down and whispered, "Back soon." Then I patted him on the shoulder and headed for the kitchen.

I plopped down in my chair, leaned over the table, and said, "All right, he's no longer within earshot. What's up? What do you need to tell us?"

Tara stared at the table and gnawed on a thumbnail, as if she were trying to muster up courage. But for what?

A frustrated Maddie glared at Tara and let off some steam. "You may not think finding my sister is urgent at the moment, but I do. What the hell is going on around here? Louie won't talk and seems scared out of his mind. My sister's vanished ... Oh for shit's sake, woman! Speak to me! Now!"

Impressed, I sat back and zipped my lips.

Tara rubbed her hands together and said, "Okay, so I don't know if you even know this, but Louie lost his father a few months back."

Maddie rolled her eyes and snapped. "Of course, I know. I'm family, remember?"

"Oh right. Sorry," Tara said.

Maddie sighed. "No, I'm sorry. I shouldn't have bit your head off just now. Yes, Ginny told me Diego died in an accident while working on a friend's house."

"What did he do for work?" I asked.

"He worked for a construction company as a framer," Maddie said, "but he often did side jobs. My sister told me he fell off a roof.

She didn't go into detail, but I don't guess there was much more to tell. His death was ruled an accident. I was in Italy at the time and couldn't make it back before the funeral, which disappointed my sister. I feel like I let her down, and I'd hoped to make it up to her during this visit."

Maddie shifted her attention to Tara. "Why isn't Louie speaking?"

Tara frowned and said, "Yeah, so ... that's what I wanted to talk to you guys about. Louie hasn't said much since his dad died. Just a few words here and there to his friends. And yeah, you're right. Diego's death was ruled an accident. Anyway, so working as a framer, and with Ginny as a waitress, they could have never afforded all this"—she gestured to the grand house in general—"but he'd inherited it. And now Ginny has inherited it. Otherwise, they'd be living like Nick and me ..."

She was rambling.

I huffed a frustrated sigh and stood. "Look, Tara, thanks for coming over and talking to us about Louie. As to Ginny and Diego's financial situation, we don't care about it. Something's going on here; I'm sure of it. We need to find Ginny. So, let's go."

I realized I'd been a bit harsh with her. She didn't deserve it. But the clock was ticking. I wanted more action, less talk.

"Go where?" Tara asked, her eyes wide with apprehension.

"To Ginny's work," I said. "Right now. I want you to take me there."

Tara grabbed her phone, tossed her hair over her shoulder, and headed for the front door. "All right, sure. Let's drive over and see what they can tell us."

Maddie smiled and gave me the face she always did right before she was about to high-five me.

"Go do what you do best, Sloane," Maddie said. "I'll stay here and watch Louie."

I headed down the hall to tell Louie goodbye, wishing I could stay and help him deal with whatever he was going through. For now, it would have to wait.

6

Tara took me back down to the docks where Ginny worked as a waitress at Leo's Tavern. Turned out, Leo was the owner and was once married to one of Maddie's other sisters, Christine. They'd never had children. After their divorce, Christine had moved up north somewhere, but Leo had stayed in the area.

Leo wasn't around when we showed up. Ginny wasn't either. Melissa Walker, a waitress who worked with Ginny, said no one had seen Ginny for hours, not since her shift ended earlier that afternoon. Tara and I went around back and checked the tavern's parking lot for Ginny's car. It wasn't there.

It didn't make any sense.

Where was she?

Tara offered to stay the night with Louie, and I declined her offer. Sure, she was a close family friend, but I didn't know her, and until I could figure out what was going on with Louie, I was hesitant to leave him alone with anyone. I knew Maddie would agree.

We pulled back into Ginny's driveway, and Maddie walked out of the house to meet us.

"Any sign of my sister?" she asked.

"Nope," I said. "Either no one knows where she is, or if they do, they're not talking."

Tara's cell phone rang. She stared at the name of the person calling and sat for a moment, not answering the phone. I peeked at her screen. The name on the caller ID was Leo, and the look on Tara's face said she didn't want to talk to him. Reluctant, she put the phone to her ear and listened to what Leo had to say. Then she said, "Umm ... hold on," and turned toward me. "Uncle Leo heard we stopped by the tavern looking for Ginny. He's concerned. He wants to come by to see Louie. He doesn't sound happy."

Her voice was shaky, her tone worrisome.

Why did I get the impression a visit from Uncle Leo was a bad idea?

"Tell him I'm a friend of Louie's aunt Madison," I said, "and until we figure out what's going on, the answer is no."

Tara flattened a hand over the phone's speaker and whispered, "Umm ... no one tells Leo *no*."

"I just did."

"That's just ... well, crazy. You don't know him like I do, and—"

I jerked my cell phone out of my handbag. "This whole thing is crazy, and since we're not getting anywhere, I'm calling the cops."

It wasn't what I wanted to do just yet, but I was done remaining at square one. I was worried about the boy. I was worried about Maddie's sister. And I was worried about Maddie.

Maddie grabbed the phone out of my hand and shook her head. "Let's wait a minute before we call the police."

"Why?" I asked.

"Let's give her a little bit longer to turn up first. I'm hoping Ginny has a good explanation for all this. Plus, she's ... ahh, had some run-ins with law enforcement in the past. It was several years back, long before she got married and had Louie. Still, the cops could accuse her of abandoning her child, and I don't want to get her in trouble."

"Fine, we'll wait. The cops won't be keen on looking for her until she's been missing for over twenty-four hours anyway."

Tara said something to Uncle Leo I couldn't make out. I tapped her on the shoulder. "Ask him if he has any idea where Ginny is right now."

"I, uhh … yeah. Okay."

She asked, and Leo hung up on her.

"I'm guessing he's on his way over here," Tara said with a shrug. "It doesn't matter if you said no or not. He'll show up if he wants to show up. Yeah, so … I'm gonna go. You sure you don't want Louie to stay at my house tonight?"

Maddie and I shook our heads.

Tara slipped back into her car and said goodbye, asking us to give her a call as soon as we heard from Ginny. Tara headed down the road, and I exchanged glances with Maddie. Neither of us seemed to know what direction to go in—not at the moment anyway. We were much too tired, too stressed, and too damn hot to make sense of it all.

If Leo wanted to defy my wishes and come to the house, fine.

I'd be ready and waiting for him when he did.

7

While we waited to see if Leo would show or not, Maddie gave me the rundown on what she knew about him. It seemed Uncle Leo was a complete jerk who used to abuse Maddie's sister, Christine. The abuse was both verbal and physical. That was the reason Christine had hightailed it out of the state and the marriage some time ago. From the sounds of it, she'd made a smart move. Now I hoped he'd show. I was eager to meet Mr. Leo Fratnik.

When a car rolled to a stop in the driveway outside, we were all sitting in the living room, attempting to focus on a game of Candyland. Maddie sprang from her seat and went to the window.

"Is it Ginny?" I asked.

She sighed and shook her head. "It's Leo."

Louie looked toward the front door and wrapped his arms around himself, making me wonder if something was going on between Louie and Leo.

Had Leo hurt the boy in the past?

Or perhaps his mother even?

I patted the couch cushion next to me. "Come over here and sit by me, Louie."

He didn't hesitate to squeeze in next to me.

Maddie plopped back down on the other side of him and put a protective arm around his shoulders. "There's nothing to worry about. We're here, and we're not going to let anything happen to you, okay?"

I headed to the front door and showed Leo inside. He was a large man, imposing in not just his size but also his demeanor. I could smell liquor on his breath, slithering between a set of mammoth-sized teeth. I found myself jerking backward, repulsed, and hoped my face didn't show it.

Leo did little in the way of acknowledging Maddie or me, and instead focused in on Louie. He knelt in front of the coffee table, and Louie flinched.

"Do you know where your mom is, boy?" Leo asked.

No words.

Leo pressed on.

"You must know something, huh? Why don't you tell me what you know?"

I sat back down next to Louie and swung an arm across his chest, leaning in front of him like a human shield.

"Why don't *you* tell us what *you* know?" I countered. "Why are you interrogating Louie? It seems he's had the wits scared out of him today. You showing up here and getting in his face is making things worse."

Leo reeled back. He wasn't used to being talked to in this way, and it showed.

"And you are?" he asked.

"I'm the one who said you couldn't see Louie, and yet, here you are."

He chuckled and pushed himself up to a standing position. "You're not family, and you're in no position to tell me what to do. You have no business here."

Maddie jumped to my defense. "Leo, just shut it, okay? We have nothing to say to you, and Louie can't even speak right now because he's so shaken up about *something*. Do you know what that is, maybe?"

"Sorry to disappoint, but I don't."

She glared at him. "Then you can just leave."

"I'll leave when I'm ready to leave. I'm the boy's uncle and—"

Maddie twirled a finger into the air and escalated her tone. "I want you out of this house—*now*."

Leo's demeanor softened, and he stepped back, grinning, his arms splayed. "All right, all right. I understand. Louie is upset. Now is not the time."

He headed toward the door and turned back. "I'll check in with you later, Louie. Don't worry about your mom. I'm sure she'll show up. Always does. And hey, maybe I'll swing by and pick you up tomorrow, and we'll go to the beach."

Like hell he would.

8

After much deliberation, Maddie and I decided to take Louie back to the inn with us for the night. Our luggage was still there, it was late, and we were too tired to pack up everything we'd unpacked earlier. In the hopes Ginny would return home during the night, we left a note for her on the refrigerator, and headed to the inn.

We set up a cot for Louie when we arrived, turned on cartoons for him to watch, and headed downstairs. Lynn greeted us when we entered the kitchen. "Well, hello, ladies. Have you saved room for a slice of pie?"

"I was hoping to snag a piece for Maddie's nephew, if it's all right," I said. "Thanks again for letting him stay here with us."

"You betcha."

She sliced a piece of pie, plated it, and handed it to me along with a fork.

"Thanks," I said. "We're going to head back to our room and get some sleep. We're wiped out after such a long day."

Lynn waved her hand in the air. "Oh, goodness, of course you are! Go! Go and enjoy the comfort of our little inn. I'll perhaps see you in the morning for some loukoumades. Louie will love them. I'll also have some spanakopita. Sweet dreams!"

She fluttered off, leaving me to wonder what we'd be eating for breakfast. Whatever it was, it sounded like we were in for a real treat.

My foot had just touched the first stair when Lynn stepped back into the foyer. "Oh, in case I don't see you ... Tomorrow evening is First Friday on the docks. A must-see experience, I assure you. Music, dancing, and a ridiculous amount of amazing food."

Maddie and I looked at each other and nodded. By then, I hoped the mystery surrounding Ginny's disappearance would be resolved. A night of music and dancing was just what we needed.

"I'll make you a reservation at a table," Lynn said. "They have rows and rows of tables set up outdoors representing all the different local restaurants. Music and dancing under the stars ... It's quite a show."

"Sounds perfect," Maddie said. "We'll do our best to be there. Thanks for working out the details."

"No problem. None at all."

I headed out to the front porch and gave Cade a call, telling him about the day we'd just had, the fact Maddie's sister was missing, and about how young Louie wasn't talking. He sympathized and reminded me of a similar case he'd had while he was a detective in Jackson Hole. A man had been shot and killed, and his eight-year-old daughter had witnessed it all from the cab of her father's truck. It was six months before police talked her into telling her story. For Louie's sake, I hoped his story would have a better ending, a much more positive one, one where his mother came home, and all was right in his world again.

I ended the call with Cade, climbed the stairs, and dropped onto the bed, smiling down at Louie who had fallen asleep with his arm draped around a stuffed dolphin. I closed my eyes and thought about what Lynn had said about all the different restaurants being represented at the First Friday event.

If Ginny wasn't found by then, perhaps Leo's Tavern would have a table at the event, and I could ask Leo's group some more questions.

9

Lynn was in the kitchen the next morning, humming as she prepared us a second round of food, even though we'd had enough to keep us stuffed for the entire day. The woman was a machine. Tara called the next morning, and the first thing out of her mouth was to tell us Leo had called again and was coming over.

I threw my hands in the air and stared down at the cell phone. "What is it with you?"

"I know, I know," she said. "I shouldn't have answered the phone when he called."

"You still haven't heard from Ginny, right?"

"Sorry, I haven't. I'm worried. She wouldn't take off like this without telling me first, and she'd never leave without her son."

Maddie and I shared a worried glance.

"Look, we'll keep Louie until she's found," I said. "Thanks for calling to check in. Let us know if you hear anything new, okay? We'll do the same."

The call ended, and I glanced at Louie, who'd been picking at the same bowl of fruit for the last fifteen minutes. It was time for a straight-up quiz. "Do you want to see Uncle Leo, or maybe go to the beach with him today?"

He shook his head.

"Do you like your uncle?"

Another shake of the head.

"Does he scare you?"

A nod.

Lynn entered the room. I pulled her aside and explained our desire to stay with Louie but in his own environment.

"We'll be checking out until his mom comes home or until we know something at least," I said. "It's about time to involve the police too."

I turned to see Maddie wiping a tear from her eye, and I hugged her. She always preferred to see the world as nothing but butterflies and rainbows, despite the fact she knew otherwise.

"You ladies do what you need to do," Lynn said. "No worries here. Let me know if I can help, and here"—she handed Maddie two tickets—"these will get you seats for a First Friday dinner on the docks. You can bring the boy, no charge. Leo's Tavern has amazing food."

And just like that ... we were being seated just where I wanted to be.

10

"Bye, Louie. We won't be long. Just a quick errand we need to run," Maddie said as she gave her nephew a big squeeze. The purple and pink tie-dyed dress she wore, with its big sleeves and loose fit, almost covered the kid as he hugged her back.

Lynn had offered to watch Louie while we went to the police station. Having seen some of the games and toys she had stuffed around the inn, he agreed to stay until we returned. He also seemed comfortable in Lynn's presence, which made the decision to leave him with her a lot easier.

While some law enforcement buildings could be bland and imposing, the Tarpon Springs Police Department was modern and even welcoming. The roar of US 19 could be heard in the distance. I was pleased not to have to drive on that nutcase highway. The smaller roads inside the town kept my anxiety levels at a low—there was beauty everywhere you looked, it seemed—and we needed that right now.

We stepped inside the police station, told the girl at the front desk why we were there, and waited for assistance. About thirty minutes later, a door opened, and an officer waved us back.

"I'm Detective Kyle Flint. Understand you want to file a missing persons report?"

"We do," I said.

"I apologize for the wait. We're a little short-staffed today."

"No problem," I said, even though the wait had been frustrating. In fact, Maddie and I had both been on edge as we watched the minutes tick by on the giant clock in the lobby area.

We settled at the detective's desk, and he pulled up a form on his computer. "Your names, please?"

We told him, including our contact info, occupations, and the fact that we were here on vacation. He typed as we spoke.

"And the person who is missing?" he asked.

"My sister, Ginny Alvarez," Maddie said. "Ginny's a caring, sweet person. I know she wouldn't leave her son high and dry."

He sat back in his chair. "No kidding. I know Ginny. Shame about her husband."

"It is. Yes," Maddie whispered.

There were a few beats of uncomfortable silence that I chose to break. "If I may," I looked at Maddie, who nodded. "Here's what we know ... and what we don't know."

It was an easy task because at the moment, we knew so little.

Ginny was missing.

Louie wasn't talking.

There was a man who'd been chasing after Louie.

And then there was the imposing Uncle Leo, a man I was certain couldn't be trusted.

I finished with, "We aren't sure why Louie was so scared when we found him yesterday or where Ginny might be. She's been missing twenty-four hours now, and we felt it was time to involve the police."

Flint listened, nodded, typed, and jotted down notes, and he seemed engaged while doing it, which gave me a sense of relief.

Unable to resist, I reached over and adjusted the stapler, tape dispenser, and cup of pens, aligning them next to each other on Flint's desk. OCD now in check, I leaned back and smiled.

"Okay, ladies," Flint said, pushing back from his desk. "We'll start with some inquiries at Leo's Tavern since Ginny was working there yesterday, according to ... who was it again?"

"Tara Simmons and a couple of employees at Leo's Tavern."

He snapped his fingers and looked at his notes again. "Right. Tara was listed as someone to contact in case of emergency, correct?"

"Correct," Maddie said. "She and Ginny are close friends."

"And Louie's with Lynn at the inn right now?"

"Yes," I said. "After this, we're heading right back there to pick him up."

"We're going to stay with him at my sister's house," Maddie added.

Another nod from Flint, who seemed satisfied that Louie was being well cared-for between us, Tara, and Lynn.

"We'll keep you posted," he said. "I hope it's something simple, and we'll have this wrapped up in no time."

"Is there anything I can do to help? I've been a private investigator for over ten years. I've worked countless missing persons cases before. Homicides too. Just point me in whatever direction you'd like me to go."

"I appreciate it, Ms. Monroe. But no need. Like I said, we'll be in touch. Just take care of Louie until we find Ginny, okay?"

He reached out to shake our hands, and we obliged.

As we headed out of the station and toward our car, Maddie said, "You're not going to stand on the sidelines and do nothing, are you?"

It was more of a statement than a question. She knew me well.

I raised a brow and grinned at her. "Not a chance."

11

The First Friday dock party, dubbed "A Night in the Islands," didn't start until later in the day, and Louie seemed to be in desperate need of a distraction. Without any good leads for me to follow yet, Maddie and I decided a break from his current troubles might be just what he needed right now. It was what I needed too—time to figure out my next move—leads or no leads. I needed a game plan to get Louie to start talking. As much as I loved the idea of a vacation, it was time for me to put my investigator cap on and figure out what the hell was going on with his mother.

Tara called to check on the status of things as we headed out the door, and then she invited herself and her husband to join us. She seemed nice enough, but she was starting to get on my nerves. Maybe it was because I'd wanted her to know so much more than she did. It wasn't her fault that she didn't.

We pulled into the parking lot of a glorious beach just down from the local schools. The setting was so peaceful with cascading palm trees bending over a cozy stretch of sand. It wasn't busy either. It felt like we had the whole place to ourselves, save for a few wild ones on the far left side where the boat launch was. Some para-sailers were doing impressive tricks to the right of us. Lots of walkers. The occasional older man passed by wearing tiny swimwear and a tan so dark, the skin looked charred. It caused me to adjust my wide-brimmed straw hat as I was reminded just how brutal the Florida sun could be.

"I would never be at school with a beach like this just down the street," Maddie said.

I had to agree. I'd connected with this tiny slice of heaven called Sunset Beach and felt my shoulders relax for the first time since meeting Louie. I imagined it was a normal vacation, and that no one was sad or missing ... or maybe even something far more sinister. I looked at Louie, so cute in his yellow swim trunks that went down past his knees. He was making a beeline for the water, boogie board in hand. I wasn't far behind him. I had some bonding and trust-building to do.

Louie and I played around along the shoreline, him seeming to prefer to stay in the shallow waters. Fine by me. I looked for shells and other weird items stuck in the seaweed and even found a horseshoe crab shell. I didn't dare pick it up. It wasn't long before thirst got the better of us, and we plowed through the hot sand to our blanket grouping.

Maddie held a root beer out to me. "Can I interest you in something cold?"

I nodded. "And I'll take another one for the little guy."

I grinned at him, and he put his hands on his hips and puffed out his chest.

"Ahh, not so little, then," I teased.

Maddie laughed and cracked the tab on his soda. Louie took it and gulped it down, and then ran back to the edge of the water, attempting "big moves" on his board.

"How's the bonding going?" Maddie asked. "He say anything to you yet?"

"Nope. Not a word."

Tara walked up, introduced Nick to us, and they both sat down.

"Thanks for letting us join you today," Tara said.

"I'm guessing the reason you asked to come along today is because you don't know us and you're worried about Louie," I said. "Am I right?"

"I ..." Tara hesitated a moment and then said, "You're right. I don't know you, and the fact Ginny is still missing is freaking me out."

"I'm freaked out too," Maddie said. "But you don't need to worry. Louie's safe with us."

Tara grinned like she wanted to believe us but still needed to be convinced. I didn't blame her. She was like a second mother to Louie.

"It's great that you're taking such an interest in him," Nick said, then added in a lower voice, "And I'm glad to hear you've been keeping him out of his uncle's grasp."

"I take it you don't like Leo much, eh?" I asked.

Tara snorted out a laugh, and Nick chuckled. "Not a bit. The guy's kinda strange. I'm just glad I don't run into him much."

"We avoid his tavern like the plague," Tara said.

I needed to find out more about Leo Fratnik, and fast. Something was off about him. I felt it in my bones. But whom could I ask?

I looked over the small sand dune to see Louie still working his board. He was one person who could tell me about Leo Fratnik. There was just one problem—he still wasn't talking.

A muscular, tanned man with a broad smile and a set of bright, polished teeth approached our group and looked at Nick. "Yo, Nicky. Where ya been?"

Nick stood, and the two slapped hands, followed by a quick bro hug. He gestured toward us gals. "Just hanging out at the beach."

The beefy guy glanced at Maddie and me, and Nick said, "Dom, this is Maddie and Sloane. They're here on vacation. Maddie is Louie Alvarez's aunt. Gals, this is Dom Andino."

Dom nodded at us and said, "Nice to meet you ladies. Hello, Tara."

Tara giggled and waved. "Good to see you, Dom."

"You out here with the boat?" Nick asked.

"We are. You guys should come over and take a spin on the jet ski. We got all kinds of toys out here today."

Nick's eyes landed on Louie at the shoreline. "Not so sure that's a great idea right now, man."

Dom frowned. "What's going on?"

"We can't find Ginny."

"Say what?"

Tara jumped in with a wave of her hand. "Long story. Maybe we shouldn't get into it right now, Nick."

Nick shrugged. "I suppose." He slapped Dom on the back. "Another time."

"Aww, come on. We haven't hung out in weeks."

Seemed like Dom "the Adonis" Andino wasn't taking no for an answer.

Eyebrows raised, Nick turned to Tara as if seeking her approval.

She smiled and said, "It's okay, sweetie. Go and have some fun. It's good to see Louie happy. I'd like to stay a while."

Dom's expression brightened, as did Nick's.

"Sounds good to me," Nick said and then turned to his buddy. "Lead the way, maestro. I'm right behind you."

And off they went for some bro time.

From what I'd seen so far, Nick was a standup guy, and I was glad Louie had him and Tara, two people who seemed like upbeat role models in his life. Even if Tara was a bit on the flaky side, it was clear she cared for Louie.

For the next hour, we lay on the blankets, chatting, and I picked Tara's brain about Ginny. Tara said she and Ginny were good friends until Ginny's husband died. In recent months, Ginny hadn't contacted Tara as much as she had before. Calls were left unreturned, and when they did get together, Ginny was distracted. Maddie's interactions with Ginny on the phone had been similar. I wondered if Ginny's change in demeanor was over losing her husband, or if there was something else going on—something she *hadn't* shared with family and friends.

Without the foresight to pack a beach umbrella, the sun's scorching heat beat down, and we were soon drenched in sweat. I'd had enough. I looked at my watch, then at Maddie. "You're starting to burn, and if you are, I must be too."

"Snowbirds, you two." Tara laughed. "You get used to it after a while."

Maddie sat up and checked her tan line, which looked a lot more like a ruby-red burn line to me. "You're right, Sloane. We should wrap things up here."

Tara pointed at the boat ramp, where Nick's booming voice could be heard over the others as he rode the jet ski like a maniac around the nearby waters. "I'm going to head over and make sure he's not getting into too much trouble."

"Good call," I said.

While she headed over, I watched Nick for a few seconds as he did tricks on the jet ski. I couldn't help but wince. He was far braver than I'd ever been on the rare occasion when I'd ridden one of those things.

Maddie and I packed up, and I waved at Louie, who was digging holes in the sand. "Five minutes and then we're leaving, okay?"

He nodded, and then a blood-curdling scream ripped through the sticky, coastal air. A scream that intense always meant the same thing—something horrible had just happened.

12

I whipped my head around and saw Tara running toward the boat ramp at full throttle, wailing, "No, no, no!"

I turned my attention back to Louie, who had just looked up, curious about the mayhem that was unfolding. *What to do, what to do?*

Maddie looked at me and said, "I got him."

"Take him away from here," I said. "I'll hang back and see what's happened."

Maddie nodded, took Louie's hand, and headed toward the car. Once he was secured inside, and Maddie had started the car, I broke into a jog and headed over to Tara, who was on her knees on the shoreline, sobbing. Nick was face up in the water, unmoving, being dragged to shore by several men.

I leaned down and placed a hand on Tara's shoulder. "What happened?"

She shook her head, unable to speak.

"I'll be right back," I said.

I sloshed through the water, meeting the men partway. A guy with a snake-and-dagger tattoo covering his entire right arm was holding Nick's shoulders above water. I looked at him and said, "What's going on? What happened?"

He shrugged, as did the other two men who were holding on to Nick.

Dom jogged up with a cell phone to his ear. He looked at me and said, "Nick hit the anchor line, right across the neck. I'm on with 9-1-1 now."

I turned to see Tara next to me, urging her husband to wake up. It was to no avail.

"Help is on the way," I said. "Try to stay calm, okay?"

Eyes wide, she nodded, while she nibbled on one of her freshly manicured pastel-green fingernails, which matched her two-piece suit. She wrapped her arms around her body, shivering. There was no way she'd find a sense of calm, not yet. But at least she wasn't wailing.

I shifted my focus to Dom and whispered, "Is he breathing? Does he have a pulse?"

He shrugged in response as he choked on whatever words he was trying to get out. I leaned in closer and inspected Nick. How hadn't he seen the anchor line? With all his antics, my worst fear had come true. He had hit both something and someone—the rope *and* himself. And the marks on his neck and face indicated it was one hell of a hit.

Unable to resist, I reached out and felt for a pulse.

I had to know for sure.

There wasn't one.

13

The ambulance arrived and made haste as they loaded Nick into the back of the vehicle. Tara was right by his side, eyes red, the expression on her face a combination of panic and despair.

Before they took off, I grabbed one of the EMTs by the arm and whispered, "Hey, back there ... I tried to take his pulse. I couldn't find one."

He gave me an awkward smile and said, "I'm sorry, ma'am. I can't talk about his medical situation with you."

I knew he couldn't, but it had been worth a shot at least.

A second EMT popped her head out of the back of the van and motioned for me to come over. I approached her, and she said, "He's got a pulse, but it's faint."

The EMT closed the ambulance door, and I breathed a sigh of relief. The ambulance whined as it headed down the road. I waited until it was out of sight and then ordered a taxi to drop me off at the inn. While I waited for it to arrive, I thought about something Maddie had said to the detective who had taken our missing persons report earlier that morning.

"Ginny's a caring, sweet person," she'd said. "I know she wouldn't leave her son high and dry."

If true, it was hard not to suspect the worst. Ginny had been gone far too long without making contact. I'd never raised a child, but mothers just didn't leave their kids alone this long without a good explanation.

The taxi pulled curbside, and I arrived back at the inn soon after to find Louie being entertained by Lynn and her arsenal of kid-friendly activities. Maddie approached me. She looked even more worried than before, something I wasn't used to seeing.

"What happened at the beach?" she asked. "Is everyone okay?"

I filled her in on Nick's accident.

"Sheesh," she said. "I hope he's all right."

I did too.

"I wish Louie would start talking," I said.

"He's terrified of something, Sloane. I've never known him to act like this. When I video-chatted with him in the past, he was a chatterbox. How he's being now, is ... well, bizarre to say the least."

"I have an idea. Why don't we ask Lynn if she'll help us make some flyers? We can spread them around the city and maybe get a tip on Ginny's whereabouts."

Lynn loaned us her computer, and we created the flyer, printing out a small stack. For the next hour, Maddie and I walked the streets along the docks, while Lynn sat at an ice cream shop with Louie. We showed Ginny's photo to passersby and stapled and taped the flyers wherever we could. We hoped someone somewhere knew something. But it seemed no one did.

Exhausted and still not packed, we returned to the inn, showered, and debated whether or not to attend the First Friday dinner shindig. My body screamed to skip it, to relax and reset so I'd be fresh and ready to try again tomorrow. My conscience, however, had a different opinion. Since we'd been assigned to a table at Leo's restaurant, it was the perfect opportunity to interrogate Ginny's coworkers again—with a lot more force this time, if necessary.

I sat Louie down and asked if he'd like to come to dinner with us.

He shook his head, yawned, and rubbed his eyes, indicating he didn't want to go. I couldn't help but wonder if it was all a show on his part. Was there something at the docks that frightened him? I felt sure of it, given what I'd witnessed so far. But what?

Lynn, who'd overheard my conversation with Louie, offered to babysit once more. I was hesitant to leave him alone again, but at the same time, I needed a break from the tension—and even more important, a break in the mystery of Ginny's disappearance. By now, Lynn was aware of everything going on, and she wanted answers just as much as we did. She suggested we stay at the inn one more night instead of heading to Ginny's like we'd planned. Given the hour, it was a logical choice.

On our way to dinner, Maddie and I made a quick stop at Ginny's house, just in case she'd shown up there or left any evidence of having been there since we'd left. We found nothing to suggest she'd been there. Disappointed, we headed for the docks. I knew other cities hosted First Friday events, but this one was unique, focusing on the traditions of Greece and this town. I was intrigued. "A Night in the Islands" seemed like a perfect way to describe it.

We parked and followed the sounds of the crowd. As we emerged onto the main drag, I gasped at the wonderment in front of me. Rows and rows of tables were set up waterfront, shrimping boats, sponge boats, and fishing boats all lined up behind them. There were twinkling lights and candles everywhere, and the stars had come out with their own display of beauty.

A Greek band decked out in Greek attire played the exotic rhythm of their music. It was all so charming in an old-world way. I couldn't believe how much it had transformed from when I'd been there the day before. It no longer looked touristy, and instead catered to locals, with family and friends gathering to cut loose on a special night.

We arrived at our assigned table, placed our orders—Leo's served Greek/American cuisine—and sat back, plastic wineglasses filled to the rim. The music and the murmurs of a happy crowd almost made me forget I had a case to solve. The longer I sat, the more I relaxed. I looked over at Maddie, whose arms were raised high in the air, swaying to the rhythm of the live Greek music.

While I had dressed in a simple lilac shift, Maddie wore a white sundress with delicate lace details, a sharp contrast to her tan/burn. Her braid had been neatened, and she wore just a hint of makeup on her face. She looked happy and like she had forgotten her troubles for the moment. I didn't want it to end.

"Let's go dance," she said, pointing to a few people out on the street in front of the band.

Dancing had never been my strong suit. I shook my head and said, "I think not."

My response didn't go over well.

Maddie dragged me from my seat, removed the wineglass from my hand, and said, "Let's go. They're doing that Greek dance thing."

"Can we eat first at least?" I begged. "I'm starving."

I blinked at her, wondering how she found the energy to dance after the day we'd had.

She gave me a pouty look and said, "Oh, fine. After we eat though, we're dancing the stress away, even if it's just for a few minutes. I need to get my mind off all of this ... this heaviness I'm feeling right now. Got it?"

I agreed, breathed a sigh of relief, and we sat back down. Our food arrived minutes later, and we hunkered down to eat. The gyro I'd ordered was the best I'd ever had. The flaming cheese and vegetable moussaka were equally scrumptious. Maddie and I were picking off each other's plates like scavenger seagulls. I rubbed my stomach and pondered whether I had enough room left to finish my wine.

I took a sip. *Yep, there's room, but not much.*

I heard a roar of laughter and looked over at the next table, where a large group had congregated. My eyes landed on one man in particular—the man I'd seen chasing Louie the day before.

His eyes met mine, and he scanned my face as if trying to place where he'd seen me before. Reality hit a moment later, and he rose from the table, his speed picking up as he headed away from the festivities and into the shadows of the night.

It was suspicious.

Too suspicious.

I bolted from my chair and made my way in his direction.

He wasn't getting away—not this time.

14

Maddie's voice echoed behind me. "Hey, wait up. Where are you going?"

I held a finger up and kept on moving.

So did the man.

There was no doubt in my mind now—he'd recognized me.

He weaved between several groups of people and broke into a light jog, glancing over his shoulder every now and then to see if I was still there.

To his chagrin, I was close behind, mirroring his every move.

We had moved away from the crowd now, and that emboldened me. I grabbed a conch shell I found lying by itself on the sidewalk and threw it as hard as I could. I nailed the guy in the back of the head. He yelped in pain and stumbled toward the ground but was back on his feet again before I could grab him.

Now he was running.

I tore after him, weaving between people and objects like I was the wind. The distance between us narrowed. The moment he got within my grasp, I drew my martial arts card. I reached down, wrapped my hands around one of his legs, and jerked it off the ground. He toppled over, faceplanting on the cement.

Maddie pulled up beside us. I looked up at her and said, "Help me hold him down."

Confused, she nodded and did as I asked.

I turned my attention back to the man, a slender slip of a thing, nothing more than skin and bones. He had spittle all over his goatee, which was streaked with gray, and dark, shifty eyes.

I bent over him. "Why are you running?"

He shared what I guessed was a Greek curse word in response.

Nice.

"Sloane, what's going on?" Maddie asked. "Who is this guy?"

"This is the man who was following Louie yesterday."

She narrowed her eyes, glared at the man, and then knelt in front of him. "Answer Sloane's question. Who are you? Why are running from her? Why were you chasing Louie?"

More swearing.

Maddie snapped her hand back and then whacked the guy across his left cheek. "Tell us what we want to know!" she screamed. "What did you do to Louie? Where's his mother? Where's my sister!"

He said nothing, and she slapped him again, on his right cheek this time. I was tempted to allow the slapfest to continue, but the second time she'd struck him was a lot harder than the first. If he didn't start talking, chances were she'd up her game and turn him into her own personal punching bag.

I placed a hand on Maddie's shoulder. "That's enough."

She backed off and looked at me like the guy had a minute to start talking or she'd finish what she started.

"Why were you running?" I asked again. "What did you want with Louie yesterday?"

He opened his eyes and glared at me. "Yo, talk to Leo. I'm too old for this shit."

Although I'd chased him away from the main event of the evening, we'd started attracting a crowd, and I noticed a cop heading in our direction. I backed away, letting the man get up. He saw the cop and reached for my hand, giving me a fake grin as he shook it. It seemed he didn't want trouble with law enforcement any more than I did.

Maddie took my arm, and we headed back to our table, intent on locating Leo. We found him huddled far back in one corner, sitting on the concrete berm near his tavern's tables, his back to the boats, watching the buzz of activity from the sidelines. I pointed him out, and Maddie made a beeline in his direction.

She reached him before I did and shoved him in the shoulder. "What's going on with you and Louie?"

He grinned and said, "Hello, Maddie. I hope you are enjoying the food, yes?"

Maddie stood her ground. "Answer me."

"Answer her," I said. "Your thug over there"—I gestured to the table where the skinny guy had returned—"we just had a nice chat. He told me to talk to you about why he was chasing Louie yesterday. I presume you have some beef with the kid. Maybe his mom too. Is that why she's missing? Hmmm?"

I crossed my arms and waited for his response.

Leo's head flopped back, and he laughed. "Ah, I see you've met Frank, a good friend of mine. Usually he's a loyal man, but I see he's given me up, so to speak." His eyes narrowed, and he glared at us. "I will have no such conversation with you ... or you, Maddie. This is ridiculous. Louie is my nephew—"

"He's *my* nephew by blood, not yours!" Maddie shouted.

Leo continued, unfazed. "There's no need to worry as you are, Maddie. Believe me. I want what's best for the kid just as much as you do. Louie is a young boy. Boys get into mischief. It is nothing more than that. I will talk to him."

Like hell you will ...

I held up a hand. "No need. If you won't talk to us, I guess we'll just have to update the missing persons report we filed today and ask the police to investigate you too."

He shrugged. "Do what you must."

"Ginny works for you," I said. "As of right now, she was last seen yesterday at *your* place, working."

He shrugged again, grabbing a toothpick from his pocket and twisting it between his lips. "I know nothing about Ginny's whereabouts. She left me high and dry today when she failed to show up for her shift. I'm not happy about that. When she does turn up, she'd better have a damn good explanation for where she's been."

"Has she ever done anything like this before?"

"Not to me." He splayed his arms. "Look, ladies, I want to help. Why don't I talk to Louie? Maybe he'll tell me what he knows."

"What makes you think he'll talk to you at all?" I asked. "From what I've seen, he doesn't like you much."

"Of course he does," Leo said.

Maddie crossed her arms and glared at Leo. "He *doesn't* like you. I can't say I blame him. I don't like you either. Never have."

It was clear we weren't going to get anywhere with Leo and his clan, and for now, I was done trying. If I was going to find Ginny, I needed to think of another way to do it.

"Come on, Maddie," I said. "It's getting late. We should head back to the inn."

As we turned to leave, I flipped back around and jabbed a finger at Leo. "Until Ginny's found, Louie's with us. Stay away from him."

15

I was restless most of the night, glancing over at Louie and then at Maddie—worried for both of them and trying to figure out what was going on with her sister. The detective side of me couldn't shut down no matter how hard I tried.

The two of them, however, had slept like the ...

Like a rock. A rock.

I couldn't finish the other phrase without a sense of panic setting in. How safe were they? Was Maddie's family in peril? They'd already lost Diego to a freak accident. How much more bad news could they take?

I was desperate to find answers so the healing could begin. I owed that much to my friend. And to Louie, who had woken at dawn and was already downstairs hanging out with Lynn, the child whisperer. The more I got to know Louie, the more he reminded me of a boy I'd met on my first missing person's case. Sweet Oliver. His mother had been murdered, drowned outside his grandparents' lake house. I hoped a similar fate wouldn't happen to Louie.

I brushed those thoughts aside and started packing up. It was time to move in with Louie at his house until Ginny was found. I checked in with Tara, who had been glued to Nick's side at the hospital. He'd survived his brush with death and was expected to make a full recovery. It was nice to hear a bit of good news for once.

Maddie called the police station for an update on the search for Ginny. While I zipped up my suitcase and dragged it to the door, I listened in on the conversation.

"Well, what are these *good leads*, as you say?" Maddie asked. "Uh-huh ... Not what I wanted to hear, you know ... Okay ... Right."

She disconnected the call, grunted in frustration, and flung the phone on the bed.

"Nothing?" I surmised.

She rubbed her eyes, and I noticed they were red and foggy. Maybe she hadn't slept as well as I'd thought.

"Nothing. Well, maybe something. They tracked her phone to the tavern in a back room somewhere, and they're looking through that now. No car, no purse. They say they have some other good leads they're working, but they're not gonna share them with us just yet. Jerks."

"You know they can't, Maddie. Not for a while, at least."

She blew out a long sigh. "I'm family, Sloane! They have to tell me what's going on."

"Look," I started, putting my arm around her, "let's just get situated at Ginny's house, and then we can figure out something to do."

She leaned in, and my heart once again went out to her. Years ago, I'd lost my own sister. I knew what she was going through.

Another long sigh from Maddie, this one with some vocals behind it. She flailed her hands and said, "Fine. Let's get moving. But I don't see me enjoying anything about this getaway from here on out."

I couldn't blame her. She had so looked forward to our little retreat. We both had.

Then it hit me.

The cops had said they were investigating some leads, *good leads*, which meant they'd found out things I hadn't. Being in another state, one where I wasn't a licensed private investigator, I needed to be a lot more subtle when it came to nosing around. Nightfall would provide such an opportunity, and I decided to start by conducting a search of Ginny's house.

I hadn't exercised my snooping muscles for a while.

It was about time I gave them a nice stretch.

16

We relaxed for most of the day, which set my OCD tendencies aflare. Downtime always caused me to focus on even the smallest details, like the fact Ginny didn't seem to know how to hang a single picture straight in her entire house. Maddie and Louie watched TV and played video games, stopping here and there to munch on food. Their mood was subdued, their energy low. I felt for both of them.

While Maddie and Louie zoned out, I thought about what little I knew about Ginny's disappearance so far, which still wasn't much at all. It was frustrating. I needed to do better.

I knew Ginny had worked the day she went missing. No one saw her leave, but her car wasn't in the parking lot, so she must have left at some point. Yet her phone had been found in the back room. I supposed she could have just forgotten it. But wouldn't she have realized it was missing and returned right away to retrieve it?

The employees I'd questioned at the tavern had seemed flighty, not looking me in the eye when I asked about Ginny. And then there was Tara herself, who was unnerved whenever Leo was a topic of conversation. She feared him, that much was clear. And last but not least was the loyal-but-not-so-loyal Frank.

I hated this part of finding a missing person—the part where I had too many questions and too few answers. At the same time, having a case to investigate calmed me somehow. Not because I wished ill will on anyone, but because I always felt more purposeful when I was helping others. I'd never been any good at relaxing. Not for long anyway.

There was a knock on the door, and I rushed to get it. A break in the routine. I'd take it, no matter what it was. It was a blond girl with her fine hair up in a messy bun. She was just about Louie's age.

"Can Louie play?"

I looked past her. "Did you come here by yourself?"

She nodded. "I live right there." She pointed toward the house across the street. "My mom watched me come over. I need to call her ... if I can play?" She peeked inside the house, and her pretty blue eyes lit up. "Hi, Louie!"

Louie smiled.

I thought about saying no, but how could I resist when Louie looked so happy to see her?

"What's your name?" I asked.

"Lisa. What's yours?"

"Sloane."

"Never heard anyone named Soan before."

It was close enough and had been said in far too cute of a way for me to correct her. An idea sprung to mind. Maybe I could get Lisa to tell me more about Louie, and she could get him to talk. Tara had mentioned he sometimes talked to his friends. "Come on in, Lisa." I opened the door wide. "Let's give your mom a quick call."

Maddie came to the door just as Lisa stepped in. "My how you've grown!" she cooed.

Lisa blushed and wrinkled her nose.

"Louie, you need to change out of your pajamas first," I said. He'd been wearing them all day, and I hadn't pushed him about it. "Lisa, come with us into the kitchen." I looked at Maddie and jerked my head in that direction, indicating she should follow. "We'll give your mom a call while Louie gets changed."

After Lisa had placed the call, I knelt down so I was eye level with the girl and said, "I'm friends with Louie's aunt Maddie here. We're visiting."

She blinked and said, "Okay."

"We noticed that Louie isn't talking much."

She shrugged. "He just doesn't like to talk sometimes. It doesn't matter. Playing is more fun than talking anyway."

I looked at Maddie and saw that the light bulb had gone on in her head.

"Do you think you could get him to tell you why he doesn't like to talk anymore?"

"Louie's my friend. I don't want to tattle on him or anything." Her eyes narrowed. "You don't want me to tattle, do you?"

I wouldn't have called it "tattling," but I didn't want to get into semantics with a child. "No, of course not. But if Louie is sad or if he is scared of something, then you should talk to an adult so we can help him."

She crossed her arms. "Maybe he just doesn't like adults."

Little smarty-pants.

Just then, Louie entered the room, and the questioning ceased. It had been worth a try, though I'd hoped we would have gotten a little something.

Louie grabbed a box of sidewalk chalk out of the drawer. Maddie and I watched as they went out back and decorated various surfaces with their charming art. I was struck with emotion by their innocence and ease with each other.

Maddie looked at me, and I looked at her. Tears had welled up in our eyes. We'd been thinking the same thing, I guessed.

I sniffled, gave her a quick hug. "Let's go relax while they play for a while."

"Good idea."

We settled on the couch, and Maddie turned on a Netflix series she'd been raving about.

I dozed off until it was time for Lisa to go home. Dinnertime. I kicked myself for falling asleep instead of talking to Lisa's mom in person. I should have gone over there and asked some general questions while I had the chance. The woman might know something. Too late now. I made a mental note to approach her tomorrow, along with some of Ginny's other friends and colleagues.

When nightfall arrived, I couldn't get us all to bed fast enough. Maddie took Louie for a bath and then read him a bedtime story and tucked him in. I had a glass of wine with Maddie and then convinced her that we should get to bed early so we'd be fresh for whatever tomorrow might bring. For now, I'd decided not to tell her about my plans to nose around Ginny's house. I knew she'd want to join me, and though I understood, I worked better, and faster, alone.

I waited for the sounds of deep breathing, signs that both Louie and Maddie were asleep. Maddie was easy. She always snored a little —her telltale sign. It didn't take long and ... there it was. Maddie snorted and smacked her lips. Then she turned over and did more of the same. She was out, and it was go time.

I slipped out of bed and grabbed the flashlight I'd stuffed under my pillow. After checking to make sure Louie was also sleeping, I began my search, which had a wide berth. In fact, I had no idea what I was searching for yet. All I knew was that I felt certain there were clues nestled in these walls, something that would point me in the right direction as far as where Ginny had gone and why.

After checking all drawers, cushions, and papers throughout the living areas and kitchen, I headed toward the home office and realized the door was locked. I hadn't expected it, and the implication gave me goose bumps. I decided not to read anything into it yet. Perhaps Ginny kept it locked to keep Louie out of things he had no business getting into.

The lock on the office door was an ordinary one, and no match for a credit card slid at the right angle. I didn't get it on the first try, but on the second, the door popped right open. I walked into the office and shone my flashlight around.

On the far side of the room, I spotted a black, metal filing cabinet. I walked over and pulled the top drawer open. The folder at the front contained important documents, including a life insurance policy, Ginny's passport, and Louie's birth certificate, among other things. The next several folders were labeled by year with the words *Louie Age Two, Louie Age Three*, and so on. Inside I found drawings he'd made for his mother during the various years of his life. There were dozens of them. It seemed the little tyke had a real flair for the arts.

A black mug—it looked like it had been made by Louie—rested on top of a desk in the center of the room. Pencils, pens, and markers were inside. I also noted a stack of blank paper, which matched the type of paper Louie used to create his one-of-a-kind masterpieces.

Along the back wall a bookcase housed about a hundred Harlequin historical-romance paperbacks. It seemed Ginny was an avid reader.

Disappointed I hadn't found a golden ticket, I closed the door to the office and tiptoed back toward the guest bedroom, stopping first at Louie's door. He was still sound asleep. I lifted an afghan from the bottom of the bed and pulled it over him, stopping a moment to stare at his peaceful, angelic face.

Not wanting to wake him, I took my time backing out of the room. As I did so, my bare feet brushed against a piece of paper on the floor.

Strange. I hadn't noticed it before when I'd entered the room. I bent down, picked it up, and focused my flashlight beam on the paper. It was another drawing—and a disturbing one at that. Looking it over, I knew one thing for sure: we would all be having a serious conversation tomorrow.

17

Louie and I were seated at the table after breakfast the following morning, watching Maddie pace around the kitchen. She nodded at me, and I set the drawing in front of him.

He stared down at it for a moment, then jerked his head back, looking away.

I tapped on what I believed to be a gun firing and said, "What is this, Louie? What does this mean?"

He just shrugged and looked at Charlie, gesturing for the ball of fluff to hop on his lap. Charlie landed on point, tail wagging as he snuggled into Louie.

The night before, I'd woken Maddie to share the drawing I'd discovered. When she'd shaken the cobwebs from her brain and became awake enough to interpret the drawing, I could see the realization set in as she stared at the image. She agreed that we needed to press Louie for some answers. Even if it turned out the drawing had nothing to do with his mother, it was still concerning to find a drawing of a gun under his bed. At least, I assumed he had drawn it.

"This is yours, right?" I asked. "Did you draw this?"

He nodded.

The boy was a decent artist, far ahead of others his age in skill alone.

A natural, it seemed.

Maddie walked over and said, "This is weird, Louie, okay? Why would you draw something like this? How do you even know ... I mean, how would you even know to draw something like this? Help me understand, okay?"

He remained silent, and she looked over at me and let out a huge sigh.

The pencil drawing was fairly accurate in terms of what a gun looked like. The night before, Maddie guessed he could have seen it anywhere—on TV or a video game. Maybe his mom or dad had even carried a gun and shown it to him as a teaching moment—not to mess with a gun if he were to discover one.

Who knew?

And the "shot," the gunfire itself, was a spray of lead—the pencil lead. It was easy to see that he'd pressed down harder in that area to emphasize a gun firing.

If I was going to get anything out of him, I needed to change tactics.

"Please, Louie," I begged, allowing my eyes to well up with tears and my voice to get shaky. "This is so important. We want to help you. We want to find your mom. We just want ..."

I glanced at Maddie out of the corner of my eye, and she gave me a quick thumbs-up.

Louie shot out of his seat, and Charlie fell to the floor. They both took off down the hall toward his bedroom.

"Well, it was worth a try," Maddie said.

"I guess. I feel bad. I think I upset him."

She waved a dismissive hand. "Don't feel bad. I'm sure his behavior has nothing to do with you. I mean, I get it. The kiddo doesn't want to talk. But enough is enough. I'm going to have a conversation with him. Aunt to nephew. I understand he might not feel like talking to anyone, but I'm not anyone. I'm family."

She started to head out of the kitchen but stopped when the boy and pup reentered the room. Louie had returned with a series of artwork in his hand. He laid the drawings on the table and pointed to one in particular, a picture of a woman being shot.

Now we were talking.

18

Although Louie still refused to speak, Maddie and I got the clear sense that he knew something and had heard or seen something horrific. In fact, we even made the leap that this was a picture of his mother being shot—or at least he imagined it was the reason behind her disappearance. Maddie was sure the woman in the drawing looked like Ginny. Same hairstyle. Same hair color. Same body shape.

Louie left us to pore over the drawings and went into the living room to watch TV.

"This is freaking me out," Maddie said as she toyed with her messy braid.

"I get it. I feel the same way."

"What should we do now ... show these to the cops? Would it even make a difference? It doesn't prove anything. Not yet."

She was right.

"I want to talk to Lisa's mom," I said. "What's her name?"

"Tina."

"Does she work during the day? Do you know?"

"I don't think so. Last I remember, she was a stay-at-home mom."

I hoped so.

"Maybe she'll have some insights as to where Ginny might be," I said.

A grin spread across Maddie's face. "Great idea. I should have thought of that."

"You've got enough on your plate. Leave the investigating to me. Be right back."

I crossed the street and hopped up the steps of long front porch, which was filled with rockers, plants, and tables. A pitcher of lemonade and some glasses sat next to an oversized game of checkers.

Oh, for the simple days.

I rang the bell and Lisa came to the door. "Hi, Lisa. Is your mom—"

"Mom! Soan's here to see you." Then she took off.

Kids.

A woman appeared just seconds later, wiping her hands with a towel. She was a sturdy, tall woman, and her face and coloring were a mirror image of Lisa's. We did the introduction dance, and I told her what I wanted to discuss. She suggested we sit on the porch.

She poured two glasses of lemonade and handed one to me.

"So, Ginny is missing?" Tina asked, her question one of concern.

"I was hoping you might have some ideas, to be honest. Maddie and I ended up filing a missing persons report yesterday. Ginny's been gone since Thursday afternoon."

I told her how I'd first met Louie, running without a chaperone around the docks, looking like he was afraid of something.

Tina stroked her chin as she thought. "That is strange. Ginny is such a good mother."

It seemed like she wanted to say more. I waited.

"Ever since Diego died—" She stopped, shook her head. "I feel like I'm gossiping."

"You might know something that could help us. Please continue."

She exhaled a long sigh. “Well, ever since Diego died, Ginny hasn’t been herself.”

“What do you mean?”

“She’s just all skittish, nervous. A jumpy sort of thing. Though I guess that would make sense. Her world had fallen apart. That was a tight-knit, happy family if I ever saw one.”

“Does Louie talk to you? I mean, has he talked to you since his father died?”

She shook her head. “Not a word.”

“So you think this is all just part of the mourning process—her behavior, Louie not talking?”

“I do, yes. Strange that Louie was running like his pants were on fire around the same time Ginny disappeared, right?”

“Right,” I said. “My thinking is … something he saw might be related to the reason his mom is missing.”

“Yes. It makes sense. But I don’t know what it could be.”

Tina wasn’t giving me anything new here so far.

“Unless …” she started.

My ears perked up, and I sat straighter in my seat. “Unless what?”

“Well, again this is gossip, but … I know you and Maddie just want to get to the bottom of this, investigate all avenues.”

“Have any police officers or detectives come to talk to you yet?” I asked.

She shook her head.

“You were about to say something else,” I said. “I interrupted you. I’m sorry.”

She waved a hand. “It’s fine. I was going to relay something I’d overheard through the local grapevine, so to speak.” She leaned in. “I heard Ginny was having an affair.”

I had not expected this, given the whole “happy family” comment she’d made earlier.

“Oh? For how long, with whom?”

“This I don’t know. Well, I don’t know for how long. But I do know the name of the man she was supposed to be having an affair with, if that helps."

The Holy Grail, right here.

"You have a name?"

She nodded, pursed her lips, then said, "Leo Fratnik with Leo's Tavern. She works there, as you know."

I was blown away. Speechless for a few moments. Was it possible Ginny had an affair with her sister's ex-husband?

"You've been helpful," I said. "Thank you for the lemonade."

She plucked at her shorts, nervous. "I hope I haven't said too much or misled you. It's just what I've heard."

"I understand. Whether true or not, the information you've just shared could be helpful in some way we aren't even aware of yet. I appreciate it."

"I hope you find Ginny soon."

She sounded doubtful.

I, on the other hand, had renewed hope.

I was going to nail that jerk right to the wall of his little tavern. I made a beeline for Louie's house, both excited and hesitant to tell Maddie about the supposed affair.

When I entered the house, Louie was not in the living room or the kitchen.

"Where's Louie?" I asked Maddie, who was in the kitchen shoveling a bunch of grapes into her mouth.

"Hish be-roo."

I gestured toward her mouth. "Swallow."

She did. "His bedroom."

"Okay, good. You won't believe what I found out from Tina."

Before I could say anything more, Maddie's cell phone rang. She nabbed it, took a look at the caller ID, then turned the phone around so I could see.

Leo's Tavern was calling.

Perhaps Leo's ears were burning.

"Well, pick it up," I prompted.

She did.

"Mm-hmm ... Uh-huh ... I have no clue ..."

Louie walked into the kitchen and grabbed a bag of chips from the pantry.

Maddie continued her conversation. "I don't think that's gonna be a good idea ... No, I mean I don't think he wants to ... Fine, whatever."

She ended the call and bit her lip.

We made eye contact, and I knew.

"He's coming to visit, isn't he?"

She nodded.

"When?"

"Right now," she said with a sigh. "Wants to see Louie, make sure he's okay, talk to him like he suggested doing the other night, blah blah. He also asked if Tara was here, which was strange."

"He's a strange guy," I said.

Louie approached the table and pointed at the phone, his eyes questioning.

Maddie said, "Your Uncle Leo is going to stop by ..."

Before she could even finish the explanation, Louie let out a screech—a sound so animal-like, I shuddered.

Was it possible Louie knew about the affair, if there was one?

It made sense.

Louie didn't want to see Leo, and I was inclined to scoop him up and leave the house, denying Leo an audience with any of us. Of course, I didn't want to do that. I had some questions for him regarding his relationship with Ginny. I also thought of Louie's drawings and the way he reacted every time Leo was mentioned. Perhaps bringing them together again would break Louie's silence somehow. Tough love, but I felt it would be worth it.

What *had* the little guy seen?

We waited with much anxiety in the living room, like cardboard cutouts placed on the couch, all three in a row, unmoving. As much as I didn't care for the guy, I wanted to watch him interact with Louie. Maybe I'd be able to capture an elusive detail I'd missed thus far. Or maybe Leo was innocent of all wrongdoing.

Fat chance.

He was guilty of something, if not the reason Louie's mother had disappeared. I'd seen his kind plenty of times over the years as I worked my cases, and they were all guilty in one way or another. Always sticking their fingers into bad-news pie.

After thirty minutes playing the waiting game, I urged Maddie to call the tavern to see if Leo had left yet. Turned out he had, just not in the way we expected.

Maddie dropped the phone in her lap and said, "Leo's been arrested."

"Well, I'll be ..." I muttered.

Louie jumped up from the couch and pushed back the sliding glass door to the back yard with Charlie hot on his heels. We watched him go, then tried to make a decision about what to do next.

"I'm going to head to the tavern and see what else I can find out about Leo's arrest," I said. "You okay to stay here with Louie?"

Maddie nodded, and I took off toward the docks.

The tavern was buzzing with customers when I arrived. I managed to pull a couple of employees to the side to find out why the cops had nabbed Leo. I didn't learn much, but I did receive one small nugget of affirmation: Leo had been picked up in relation to the disappearance of Ginny Alvarez.

Yes!

But it turned out he hadn't been arrested; he'd been taken in for questioning. People often misunderstood the difference, but I knew better. I chided myself for not clarifying it before I drove all the way over to the tavern. Still, I was curious why they'd taken him in. Was it as simple as his tavern having been the last place where Ginny was seen, and law enforcement wanted to clarify a few things?

Did they suspect him of being involved in her disappearance?

Maybe even responsible for it?

Had he and Ginny been in the middle of some sort of tryst, and things went awry?

They were all answers I wanted to know.

I called the station to try to get an update on Maddie's behalf. Flint remained tight-lipped and said we shouldn't worry too much about Leo. It was an odd thing to say, leading me to believe Leo may have had his hand in cops' pockets. It was either that, or they no longer considered him a suspect.

It was possible Leo was an innocent party here.

Had I been wrong about him all along?

On my way back to Louie's house, I called Maddie. She revealed Leo had just contacted her. He was on his way to Ginny's house. Looked like I might receive answers to some of my burning questions soon enough.

19

When I got to the house, Leo was already there, sitting on the couch with his feet up on the coffee table. He had a glass of iced tea in hand. Louie was on the floor, playing with some figurines and cars. He didn't even glance upward. Maddie was standing with her arms crossed at the entrance to the kitchen.

Leo grinned when he saw me, all teeth and little warmth.

Yeah, well, I feel the same way, buddy.

"The gumshoe has arrived," he said.

"Yes, I have." Not much of a comeback, but I was just getting started. I looked at Maddie. "Has Louie said anything?"

"Not a word."

"What was it Leo said to him?"

"Nothing much so far."

"I'm right here, ladies." He waved his glass in the air, then set it on the table. He crawled onto the floor with Louie. I wanted to squash him like a bug. Leo, not Louie. I moved to stand between them.

"Please get back on the couch."

"I'd like to speak to my nephew if you don't mind."

"I do mind," I said. "But if you insist, you can do it from the couch."

He did one of his *raise the hands in the air* moves and rose, kneeling down next to Louie on the floor. "Louie, you seem frightened. And of course, we all understand why you're scared. Your mom is missing, your father passed away ..."

"Cripes, Leo, can we not go there?" Maddie said.

His fake charm fell from his expression, and he glared at Maddie.

I stepped in. "Leo, maybe just focus on what Louie might have seen in the last few days. Leave his father out of it. He'd been running from the tavern when I met up with him. Frank was chasing him."

I knew Louie wouldn't talk, but I wanted to see if Leo had the ability to be what I suspected he wasn't—caring.

"Tell me why you're scared, boy," he said.

Nothing from Louie.

"Okay, you like to draw, so draw me a picture maybe."

It was a good idea.

I was impressed.

Louie got up, went to his room, and came back with some colored pencils and a pad of drawing paper. He had a defiant look on his face. He started scribbling away.

Leo rose to his feet, grinning at me and Maddie. "See, ladies? You have to know how to deal with children."

I peacocked. "Like you do?"

Maddie scoffed, "You don't know the first thing about—"

"Sloane, Maddie ... come on, ladies. Give me a break."

Louie ripped the page from his drawing pad and slapped it onto the coffee table.

It was a picture of Leo, glistening big teeth being the predominant feature, and Louie had put a big X through his face.

I couldn't help it. I started to snicker. Maddie did too.

It morphed into laughter. Then hysterical laughter.

"I don't have to put up with this shit," Leo said, heading for the door.

Good, go. And don't come back.

"Wait, wait, wait," I said, following him and fighting to control myself. "I have some other questions for you."

"You'll have to ask them between here and the moment I pull the hell out of the driveway," he said.

Can do.

"Were you having an affair with Ginny?" I asked. "Or maybe still are having an affair with her?"

He stopped in his tracks and spun around. The look on his face was a genuine expression of surprise. "Why on earth would you ask me that? How did you even come up with such a thing?"

"Just a tidbit I'd heard."

"Maybe you should let the police handle things from here on out, huh? You've filed your missing persons report, now let it be."

"You haven't addressed the issue of an alleged affair with Ginny," I said. "Is it true?"

"No, there was never, ever an affair. She came to me with some questions and concerns. She was struggling."

"Before or after Diego died?"

"Both. We spent time together, mostly at work, but never in an improper way." He rolled his eyes. "The idea itself is ..."

"Yeah, that's kind of what I thought too. *Gross*."

"Try to be nice, will you?"

I would not. "It's hard with you, Leo. You're shifty, and neither Louie nor Maddie care for you much. They mean everything to me, so their opinion matters."

"It's unfortunate they feel that way."

He seemed saddened by that thought.

Was he, or was I being tricked?

"Perhaps the gossip chain has it wrong. Perhaps there is someone else, but not you? Can you elaborate?"

He sighed and slipped into the driver's seat of his old black Porsche Carrera. "I cannot. If there was another man in Ginny's life, I don't know who it is. I doubt it though. Ginny was a good person."

I froze.

Was a good person?

Without another word, he pulled out of the driveway and took off, and I knew what I needed to do next.

20

Once Maddie and Louie tumbled into bed and fell asleep, I changed into black clothing and prepared for my date with Leo's Tavern. Knowing Maddie might awaken before my return, I slid a note onto my pillow, explaining where I'd gone. When I was at the tavern earlier, I'd noticed the hours of operation listed on the back of the menu. Closing time on Sundays was earlier than the rest of the days of the week. Still, it would be dark out and the perfect opportunity to search for clues to Ginny's disappearance.

Despite the fact that we hadn't had much time to just meander around the city, I was getting familiar with the twists and turns of this little town. I was soon pulling into the empty parking lot of Leo's Tavern. I continued on until I found a parking spot tucked away in a dark corner around the back of the building.

During my previous visit, I'd examined the locks on the tavern doors. The front door locked with a deadbolt, but there was another door along the back of the building, one not used by customers. It didn't have a deadbolt, making it easy to pick.

I slipped inside the tavern and got my bearings. I was in a hallway with several doors on either side. I was keen to check each one, but first I wanted to make sure the restaurant area and kitchen were empty and that all of the staff had left for the night.

I moved down the hallway, listening for the sounds of another human. It was eerie and quiet, but then again, it was well past closing time, not just for the tavern but for the town in general.

No humans were spotted throughout, though I did have a heart attack over a cat that swept by my feet when I peeked inside the kitchen. I double-checked that space, noticing another exit door. After making sure it was locked, and it was, I headed back to the hallway determined to find Leo's office and search it.

The first three doors in the hallway were locked. Placards indicated two of the rooms were for managers and the third was Leo's office. My eyes rested on the fourth door, the first one I'd passed upon entering the building. It was unmarked. I walked over and tested the knob. The door was locked, but it took me less than two minutes to pick.

I flicked on the light, which revealed a conference room of sorts. There was a round table with several chairs around it, a beat-up dresser along one wall, and shelves and filing cabinets on another. Liquor bottles were scattered here and there, along with glasses and mugs with just a remnant of the libations they had carried. I noticed a powerful smell of bleach, like some heavy cleaning had gone on. It piqued my curiosity for a moment ... until my eyes focused on the table.

Papers had been scattered everywhere. Some official-looking documents. Some handwritten scribbles. Some photographs.

They caught my attention.

I poked through the various items, and as I did, familiar names and faces started jumping out at me.

Ginny and Diego. Tara and Nick, and then a few others I didn't recognize. More disturbing was the fact that the official documents were insurance paperwork. Life insurance. My mind raced with the possibilities of what it could mean.

Had Leo killed Diego?

Ginny?

Had he tried to kill Nick?

If so, why?

Was Tara in trouble?

Was there a scam going on, with Leo at the helm?

Was Frank the Skinny Thug involved?

Others?

Staring at the papers now, I realized they could mean something, or they could mean nothing. But it didn't feel like nothing.

It wasn't restaurant-y paperwork, by any stretch.

I snapped several pictures of the documents with my phone.

Then, heart racing, I got my tail out of there.

21

I'd decided not to wake Maddie after I returned from my night capers at the tavern. I felt like the details could wait. Come Monday morning, though, I was ready to share.

I woke to find Maddie was already out of bed. She was a long sleeper, and it was unusual for her to rise before I did, especially now that she was retired. I could hear her voice coming from the kitchen.

I threw on a pair of jean shorts and a black tank top. Peeping out the window and into the back yard, I could see it was yet another beautiful day in Tarpon Springs. And hot. I could almost see the heat waves coming off the concrete patio.

In the kitchen, I found Louie at the table, hovered over a bowl of Count Chocula and staring at the back of the cereal box. I remembered doing that as a youngster as well, and it made me smile. I gave him a quick squeeze and looked over at Maddie.

My smile dropped like a bad joke. Clutching the house phone to her ear, she wore a stricken expression and started wobbling like she was about to lose her balance and fall. I ran over and threw my arm around her, propping her against the counter. Without saying another word, she disconnected the call.

She looked at Louie, then at me, and then tipped her head toward the sliding glass door.

"Ahh ... Louie, we're going to step out back for just a second," I said.

He nodded, and I followed Maddie outside.

As soon as the sliding glass door closed, she let the tears pooling in her eyes run free.

"Ginny's body was found," she hissed in a low voice.

She was wobbling again, so I helped her over to a cushioned lounge chair and sat across from her in a rocker.

"Okay, take a breath, and when you're ready, give me the details," I said.

"That was the police on the phone. I called them to find out—" She stopped.

I waited.

Nothing more.

"Okay," I said. "Let's start with this. Where did they find Ginny?"

"In ... in the water."

Lots of water in this city. I needed more. "Which water?"

"By the boats. By the ... seawall, the docks. In that area."

"Could she have slipped and drowned?"

Maddie shook her head.

My stomach churned. I knew what she would say next.

"Sloane, she was murdered!"

I rushed to her side, wrapping her in my arms. She folded into me like a deflated accordion.

"How?" I whispered after a few minutes.

Maddie sat up, fixed her hand into a pretend gun, and put it to her forehead. Pulled the trigger.

My thoughts shifted to Louie's drawings.

He *had* seen something.

In fact, he had seen it all.

He was in danger.

I turned toward the sliding glass door. Louie was standing there, spoon in hand. Trails of tears sparkled on his chubby cheeks.

I found myself at a loss as to how I could comfort them. Perspiring not from the heat this time, I forced myself to focus, to reach back to those moments when I had lost people near and dear to me—my own sister so many years ago. All I got was a bunch of jumbled thoughts and complete brain fog. I assumed they must have been feeling the same way now.

Instead of focusing on how to comfort them in their time of need, I focused on what I did best ... finding a killer.

22

While Maddie and Louie huddled together on the couch, I went to the guest room and made a call.

"This is Sloane Monroe, and I'm calling on behalf of Madison LaFoe. You just talked to her and gave her some disturbing news regarding her sister, Ginny Alvarez."

Flint cleared his throat. "Ahh, yes. Thanks for calling back, but it wasn't me who talked to her. We were about to head out that way to deliver the news in person, but she called here first, and ... well, another officer spilled it. Should never have happened the way it did. My deepest apologies."

I wanted to raise the roof, have that officer—whomever it was—strung up, but Flint was sincere, and this was a small town, like a close-knit family in many ways. I guessed the officers and staff were just as shook up as anyone. And, yeah, people made mistakes. I let it go.

"We need to find the killer," I said.

I knew I was stating the obvious, but I wanted to see if it was possible to lead him down the path where I'd be included in their investigation.

"I know you're a PI, Ms. Monroe."

"Just call me Sloane."

"Sure. Look, I get you want to resolve this for your friend and her family. Rest assured, so do we. And we will. But I cannot share the details of the investigation with you at this time."

I sighed.

Same old same old.

"At least tell me how you were able to find her," I said.

He cleared his throat again. "It was a tip, telling us her exact location. She'd been weighted down, ahhh, pretty good. Out there in the Anclote River."

"At the docks," I clarified.

"Correct. Well, near them. Close enough."

"And she'd been shot."

"In the head. That's what would have killed her, though our medical examiner still needs to do his job. Speaking of ..."

"Maddie will need to confirm the identity," I finished for him.

"Correct."

"Who tipped you off?"

"Can't say at this ti—"

"It was Leo Fratnik, wasn't it?"

Flint didn't respond at first. Then, he said, "Could have been."

I continued the game we'd started playing. "Let me guess. He avoided being charged with anything in return for giving up the information."

"Might have been the case."

"I could just ask him."

"You know as well as I do ... he won't tell you."

It seemed Leo had been instructed to stay mum. For his safety and for the benefit of the continued investigation.

"He didn't kill Ginny, but he knows who did," I said. "He was there. He saw it all."

"I cannot confirm this information with you."

Yet he had.

In fact, he'd been more forthcoming than he realized. He didn't have to talk to me at all. I was grateful for the small-town connections. People cared and empathized. Flint was one of them.

I then made another quick call to check in with Cade. While he'd expressed concern during our call on Friday night, he was full-tilt worried now.

"You try to get away from it all and you can't," he said. "It's like no matter where you are or what you're doing ... it has a way of finding you."

"What finds me?"

"Murder."

Cade's comment was one-hundred-percent creepy.

But he had a point.

23

Maddie made a decision to head to the morgue and identify Ginny's body alone. While it was a morbid task, it was something she was familiar with, having been a medical examiner for most of her career. And while I wanted to be with her, I understood it was something she wanted to do on her own.

Louie and I hung out in the house for a while until it became obvious he was getting antsy. I suggested we go to the back yard and throw around one of his sponge footballs, and he agreed. We headed outside with Charlie in tow. To add to the fun factor, and to keep us from overheating, I turned on the sprinkler, even though it made catching the ball a lot more challenging.

After a mild warm-up session and some aggressive moves, I got more into it than I thought I would, and I drew back for a long pass.

"Better back all the way up for this one, Louie," I said. "This will be a lot harder to catch."

He shuffled to the edge of the yard and prepared to make the play.

I let loose, gasping when I saw how far I'd missed the mark. Instead of flying toward Louie, it soared toward the sliding glass door, which was open. Maddie was standing there, and the ball nailed her right in the forehead.

She bent down, picked it up, and glared at me like she had half a mind to do to me what I'd just done to her.

"I'm so sorry," I shouted as I jogged over to her. I eyeballed the red mark on her forehead and winced. "There's a slight chance it will bruise, but it's a sponge ball. How much damage can it do?"

She pressed a hand to the afflicted area and said, "More than you think."

I switched the sprinkler off and grabbed towels for Louie and me. I handed one to him and told him to wipe himself down and to give Charlie a quick rubdown while he was at it. He did, and then Maddie made him a quick snack. He took it to the living room, giving Maddie and me the perfect chance to talk.

"I know you wanted to go to the morgue by yourself," I said. "But I feel like I should have gone with you. I should have been there for you."

"Believe me, it was better for me to go alone. I wanted time with her before the funeral and all the people ... you know, to talk with her, to let her know how much I loved her—"

She broke down, sobbing into her hands.

I stood and wrapped my arms around her shoulders. We stayed there for a while and then she looked at me and said, "I promised Ginny we'd find her killer. You have to find her killer, Sloane. You will, won't you?"

I would, and not just for Maddie. For Louie too.

"I swear to you, Maddie ... I'll find him, no matter how long it takes."

24

As much as I didn't want to leave Maddie and Louie alone, I had to find Leo Fratnik and ask him some questions of my own. Maddie walked me to the front door, a look of nervousness on her face.

"Go and find my sister's killer. Just ..." She hugged me hard. "Just be careful. I can't lose another—" She stopped and buried her head on my shoulder.

I could guess the unspoken words: *I can't lose another person in my life right now.*

Louie came up and squeezed my leg, and we all stood there for a moment in a somber group hug.

I knelt down and looked him in the eye. "You doing okay?"

He nodded.

There were no tears.

His expression was blank.

No hint of sorrow or fear or ... anything.

It broke my heart into a million pieces, realizing he'd been holding in the knowledge of his mother's death all this time. What a heavy burden for a child. I couldn't even begin to fathom it.

I stood and took in a deep breath. "All right you two. Keep these doors locked. I'll be back soon."

I drove to the docks with my adrenaline at code red. Leo was at the tavern, as I'd hoped. The place was empty, save for the staff, which was a relief because I wanted to talk to him alone. I walked up to the bar where Leo was flipping through some papers and sat down across from him. He looked up and rolled his eyes.

"What is it with you?" he asked.

"What is it with *you*? Hmmm?"

He frowned. "Is this a game you want to play? I'm not in the mood. Please leave."

"No chance, I'm a customer." I gave him the fakest smile I could muster and slapped a twenty-dollar bill down on top of the bar. "I'd like a glass of Riesling please."

He pocketed the cash, poured me a glass, and set it in front of me.

I didn't touch it.

"How did the police find Ginny?" I asked.

"Have your drink, if you like. I have nothing to say to you."

"Ah, but you do. I'm not leaving until you tell me how you're involved in Ginny's murder."

I knew he couldn't share the details with me, based on what Detective Flint had said, but it didn't mean I couldn't push his buttons.

Leo grabbed a towel and began wiping down the work surface and beer taps.

"You know who killed her," I pressed. "I know you do."

He slammed his hands on the bar, leaned over, and glared at me.

I didn't flinch.

"You need to leave," he said. "I cannot talk to you. I won't."

"Who can, then? Maybe someone in the ... *back room*?"

This got his attention.

"What are you talking about?"

"You don't talk to me, I don't talk to you," I said and took a sip of my wine.

Leo shook his fist and growled in anger, like a deranged cartoon character. "You know what you should do? Stop picking on me. Cops got me zipped up anyway. Maybe look elsewhere for a change, eh?"

Lifting my chin, I said, "Maybe I'll do just that. Want to point me in any particular direction?"

He did not. He walked away, flipping me off. Just before he turned down the hallway to the office area, I heard him mumble, "Freaking ostriches, head in the sand."

What did *that* mean?

All the way back to Louie's house, I pondered that question, thinking back on our conversation. What was I missing that was right in front of my face?

When I arrived, I was almost tackled by Louie, who surprised me with a fierce hug. I looked at Maddie, who said, "He worried about you while you were gone. I could tell."

How sweet is that?

I kissed the top of his head and said, "Aww, I missed you too, buddy."

"Hey, I worried about you too," Maddie said.

She bowed her head toward me. I couldn't help but laugh. Her usual personality was making an appearance, even if it was a fleeting one. I kissed her on the top of her head too.

I was going to ask Louie to give the adults five minutes alone, but he seemed to have no interest in leaving. I let him stay in the living room with us while I gave Maddie the rundown on my brief meeting with Leo.

"He told me to look elsewhere," I said. "And then he, uh—" I glanced at Louie, who was busy with his video games, though I assumed he was listening, nonetheless. I did the flipping-of-the-bird thing out of his line of sight.

Maddie nodded. "Ohhh. Sounds like him. Jerk."

"Yeah, and then he said something about ostriches and heads in the sand, and I'm certain he was talking about us. What do you think it means?"

"I have no idea. I'd have to think about it some more, I guess."

"It just bugs me, you know? It's like he was implying it wouldn't be hard to figure out who killed Ginny." I threw my hands in the air. "I'm not sure what he meant, though. The other night, when he made a comment about Frank giving him up when we tackled him, he tried to act like he didn't care, but he did. Maybe he's trying to direct me to Frank because Frank directed us toward him. He didn't relish the betrayal, and this is his subtle way of getting back at him. Maybe it's also why he talked to the police."

"Or it could just be Leo being an asshole."

"He does seem to be good at it," I said.

Maddie snorted out a laugh. "He's not just good. He's the king of assholes."

I heard a funny sound and turned to find Louie with a cute smile on his face, snickering. It seemed we were all in agreement.

25

I whipped up a late lunch for the three of us while Maddie spent some time on the phone, notifying family and discussing arrangements for Ginny's funeral.

Yet another friend of Louie's stopped by to see if he could play. Tommy was a lanky redhead, around ten years old, and had good manners. *Please* and *may I* and all that. I wanted Louie to have some normalcy in his life again—but because of everything going on, I had to shoo Tommy away and told him to come back another day. I hated doing it, but now wasn't the time. I tried not to notice the disappointment in Louie's eyes and vowed to make it up to him somehow.

We ate our sandwiches and pasta salad in silence, all of us exhausted in our own ways. The phone rang just as I started to clear away the dishes. Maddie looked at the caller ID. "It's Tara."

She took the call.

After a few "yups" and "uh-huhs" and then a "sure," she disconnected.

"Well?" I asked. "How's Nick?"

"He's all right. Recovering. Tara hasn't left his side since the accident. She went home this morning to shower and grab a couple of things. She asked if she could stop by and see Louie before she heads back to the hospital."

"I'm guessing she doesn't know about Ginny?"

Maddie shook her head. "After what she's been through, I thought it would be best to break the news when she stops by. Besides, I'm all talked out."

"It's understandable," I said. "We'll keep the visit brief."

I turned to Louie, realizing it wasn't the best idea to break the news about his mother in front of him. Although he knew, I wanted to spare him from hearing it again.

"Hey, Louie, does Tommy live nearby?" I asked.

He nodded.

I realized I could have been more specific and tried again. "Is his house close enough that we can walk to it?"

He nodded.

"Okay, then. I know you wanted to play with him. Maybe it would be all right for him to come over for a bit. He'll have to come here though. You all right to play with him in the back yard?"

He nodded with a little more enthusiasm.

"Let's walk to Tommy's house together and see if he's still available," I said. "Then we'll come back here. Sound good?"

He gave me a thumbs-up and we walked together, holding hands, until we arrived at Tommy's house, which was a mere two houses down. Tommy was in the front yard, and he ran to us when he saw us coming.

"Hey, Tommy," I said. "Can you play now?"

Tommy nodded and said, "Yeah, I think so."

"Let's make sure it's okay with your mom or dad first, and then we'll take you back to the house with us," I said.

"Awesome. Be right back!"

And he was, his mother in tow, an affable woman with short spiky hair and bright-blue eyes.

"Hello, I'm Maria," she said.

"I'm Sloane, friend of Louie's aunt Maddie."

"So Maddie's here, huh? I haven't seen her in ages."

I assumed she hadn't heard about Ginny either, and I wasn't going to offer up the information in front of her son. Though I did wonder if she might have some insight into Ginny's life. Perhaps I'd stop by later and see if there was anything she could tell me about the weeks prior to Ginny's death.

"I'll tell Maddie you said hi," I said. "Oh, and we'll send Tommy back in maybe an hour or so?"

"Sure, I'll be here. Enjoy your stay. Tarpon Springs is the best place to visit ... and to live. I love it here."

We said our goodbyes, and the three of us headed back, returning to the house as Tara pulled into the driveway.

Perfect timing.

The sooner we got this conversation over with, the better for Maddie. Sometimes being polite was such a drag. If it had been me, I would have told her not to come. But Maddie being Maddie ... well, here she was.

Tommy and Louie took off for the back yard, and Maddie and Tara sat on the sofa in the living room. I poured a cold glass of iced tea for each of us and joined them.

"Glad to hear Nick's doing better," Maddie said.

"Yeah, me too. The doctor said he should be able to go home in a couple days or so."

"What happened?" I asked. "Did he get distracted and didn't see the rope?"

"Something like that, I guess. He said he started feeling kind of dizzy, cut the jet ski wrong, and *bam*, there was the anchor line. He's embarrassed about the whole thing. He's never fallen off a jet ski before."

The "dizzy" comment was curious. He hadn't been drinking, and he didn't seem the type to be a drug user. Then again, I knew it was impossible to dictate a "type" when it came to drugs. Or personalities, for that matter. Maybe it was some sort of medical problem.

I decided not to pry further.

It was none of my business.

Discussions moved from Nick's recovery to Ginny's whereabouts.

"Any news on Ginny?" Tara asked.

Maddie looked at me and bit down on her lip while I dropped the bomb. "Yeah, so ... they found Ginny."

Tara had been mid-sip, then gasped, initiating a coughing fit that lasted well over a minute.

"They found her?" Tara asked. "Where? Where is she?"

Tara looked around, as if she expected Ginny to enter the room at any moment.

Maddie looked at me and shook her head, indicating she couldn't bring herself to say it. I gave her a quick nod and turned toward Tara. "I'm sorry to be the one to tell you this ... Ginny's dead."

My abrupt statement chilled the air, and silence blanketed the room.

I updated Tara on the details, including the fact that Ginny had been shot and Leo had been taken into the station for questioning and then released.

Tara started to cry. "I can't believe this. I ... no ... it can't be."

Maddie rushed over to her, and they wept together.

Being my usual self, unsure what to do or say when emotions were involved, I just sat there watching the somber scene unfold.

"I can't believe she was shot in the forehead," Tara wailed. "Who would do such a thing ... and why?"

I grabbed a box of tissues and held them out. "Here you go. I'm so sorry. I can't imagine what it would be like to lose your best friend."

We sat in silence for a couple of minutes, and I pondered whether to say something more, to mention I had reason to believe Tara's own life might be in danger. Looking at her face, I decided to hold off. It was obvious she wasn't handling the news of Ginny's death well. I didn't want to shovel anything more on her plate. Instead, I said, "I can get Louie, if you'd like to say hello."

She slapped a hand over her mouth. "Oh my gosh, Louie. How's he doing? Does he know about Ginny?"

"He knows. He's still not talking."

She stood. "Give him a big hug for me, all right?"

"You don't want to see him?" I asked.

"I do, believe me. It's just ... I can't. Not right now. I'm a mess. I wouldn't even know what to say to him. I'll stop by again tomorrow or the next day, if that's okay."

"Of course it is," Maddie said.

I stood and walked Tara to the door. "Are you sure you're okay to drive right now? I can take you back home or to the hospital."

"I'll be ... fine."

I watched her walk to the car, her head lowered, clutching the damp tissue I'd given her, and I thought of Maddie. We'd been so close for so long. If she died, I wasn't sure what I'd do, or how I'd cope. To think about it now angered me.

Someone was going to answer for all of this.

I just had to find Ginny's murderer.

And when I did, I'd make him pay.

26

While Maddie took a bath and Louie played with Tommy, I made a beeline for my room, where I could still keep an eye on Louie from the bedroom window. There I wrote out a list of the facts as I knew them.

Louie had been running from Frank the Skinny Thug, after seeing something that terrified him. Frank seemed hell-bent on catching him, and I believed he would have if I hadn't gotten in the way.

What would he have done with Louie if I hadn't been there?

I shuddered at the thought.

Louie had seen his mother being shot; he'd drawn pictures about it. The trauma of it all had scared him speechless.

I thought about the location of the tavern in relation to the moment I first saw Louie. The tavern would have been behind him as he was running.

Had Ginny been shot there?

The bleach I smelled in the locked room gave me reason to believe she had. There had been a deep cleaning of some sort. Could it have been to wash away any signs of a murder that had taken place? If Ginny had died at Leo's Tavern, who had tossed her into the river with weights on her dead body?

They were all things I needed to confirm with Flint, if he'd tell me, along with whether or not a silencer had been used, since no one had reported hearing a gunshot or any similar loud noise on the day of her disappearance.

Was it possible Frank shot Ginny?

At the start, it was easy for me to pin Ginny's murder on Leo, but now, with the knowledge he'd cut a deal, I doubted he was the killer. According to Detective Flint and based on what Leo had implied, Leo was innocent of the shooting, but maybe not innocent of the *knowledge* of the shooting.

Had Leo led the police to Frank? Were they about to arrest him at any moment for Ginny's murder? Leo and Frank had history. And despite the fact Frank had suggested I talk to Leo I wasn't convinced Leo would squeal on a close friend ... or would he if his own life was at stake?

It dawned on me Leo could have been responsible for shooting Ginny, and, knowing the police were investigating too close to home, he'd gone to the police to implicate someone else.

There were other things troubling me too.

Diego's recent death, and the fact Nick had almost bit it on the jet ski. Diego's death had been ruled an accident. Nick's brush with death seemed to be a fluke misfortune too.

But were they?

I thought about the insurance paperwork I'd seen in the back room at Leo's Tavern.

Was there some sort of scam cooking?

Whatever was cooking, I was ready to douse the fire.

I reached for my cell phone and called Flint.

"Flint here."

"Hey, this is Sloane, Maddie LaFoe's friend."

"Let me guess. You have more questions."

"I do, and I appreciate your time while I ask them," I said.

I hoped the pleasantries would keep him from cutting me off too soon.

"Go on."

"I was just wondering ... when Ginny was shot, was a silencer involved?"

Several seconds went by with no response, and for a moment, I thought he'd hung up. I looked at my cell. We were still connected. I waited.

"There *might* have been a silencer involved. We've shared very few details with anyone because—"

"I know ... because you're still in the middle of the investigation. I've been there many times. Just one more question. Did the shooting happen at Leo's Tavern?"

A long, deep sigh, and then, "It is a place of interest in our investigation."

"I see."

"How are Maddie and Louie holding up?" Flint asked.

"They're okay. I mean, they're not okay. You know?"

"I do. Please let them know the entire police force is thinking of them."

"I will."

"I know you want to help, and while I appreciate it, we're doing everything we can. Instead of investing so much time into who killed Ginny and why, be there for your friend, and let me do my job, okay?"

It wasn't okay.

But right now, if I wanted to keep our communication going, I was at his mercy.

"Yeah, sure," I said.

I ended the call and replayed the conversation in my mind. He hadn't given me much, but it was enough for this dog to have a new bone.

27

Louie and I walked Tommy home, giving me the perfect opportunity to ask Maria a few questions. I found her in the front yard pruning a hedge with a pair of garden shears. She saw us coming and headed in our direction.

"Hey, Maria, do you have a minute?" I asked.

"I always have time for a chat," she said, waving us inside. "Boys, go on and play upstairs."

When the boys were out of earshot, I said, "Thank you. I'm just curious about a few things."

She led us to the kitchen. "May I get you anything—"

"No, no. I'm good. Thank you."

We sat across from each other at the table.

"Is everything okay?" she asked.

"I'm afraid I have some bad news to share."

She pressed her fingers to her lips. "Oh no. Did something happen with the boys?"

I smiled and said, "Everything was fine. I was happy Tommy could spend some time with Louie today. It's been a difficult day to say the least."

Maria bit her lip and waited for me to say more.

I explained Ginny had been missing since Thursday, the same day Maddie and I had arrived in town. I told her how Ginny's body had been found this morning in the Anclote River. I said she'd been shot in the head, which meant she'd been murdered.

There was no easy way to say it.

Maria paled, and her eyes welled up with tears. Without warning, she bolted out of her seat and sprinted down the hall.

A door slammed.

I waited.

One minute, then two, then three.

No Maria.

I stood and headed in the direction she'd fled. The first door I came to was closed. I leaned in, listening to the sound of someone sniffling on the other side.

"Maria, are you okay?" I asked. "Can I come in?"

There was no response at first, and then the bedroom door opened. Maria looked at me through damp lashes and said, "I'm sorry. I didn't mean to take off like—"

"It's all right. There's no need to explain. What happened to Ginny ... well, it's awful. It's been a hard week for everyone who knew her."

She inhaled a long, slow breath. "Give me a minute, okay? I'll be right out."

I nodded and returned to the kitchen table. When she joined me a few minutes later, her face had been wiped clean. The makeup she'd been wearing was gone.

She took a seat and said, "Please, what else can you tell me about Ginny?"

"The police are working the case, but ... I've been a private detective for years. I've worked cases like this before, plenty of them. Because Ginny is Maddie's sister, I feel compelled to do a little investigating of my own."

She nodded. "Makes sense."

"Can you think of anyone who would want to hurt Ginny? Maybe someone she had a falling out with or any enemies she may have had?"

"Not a one. Ginny was the kindest person. She had a lot on her plate after Diego died, but she still managed to keep it together for Louie's sake."

"Were you two close?"

"Close enough, I would say. We've been neighbors for a long time, and, as you can see, our boys are good friends."

Given the shock she'd just received, I'd taken my time with my questions, tiptoeing up to the one I wanted to ask most. She seemed to pick up on my hesitation and said, "Is there something specific you want to ask me?"

Thank you for that opening, Maria.

I'll take it.

"Yes, there is." I paused, still trying to decide whether or not I should poke the bear. I put my detective cap on and went for it. "Do you have any idea if Ginny was having an affair?"

Maria's forehead collapsed into a row of folds as her eyes narrowed and her nostrils flared. She jerked her head back and spat, "How could you even ask something like that?"

I'd poked the bear, it seemed.

I held up my hands in defense. "Please. I'm not trying to start gossip. I'm trying to ... disprove something I heard."

"Someone said Ginny was having an affair?"

"Yes."

"Who?"

"I'm sorry. I can't say."

"When would she have had the time to have an affair?"

"I'm not sure when," I said. "Does the timeline even matter?"

"Who was this alleged affair with ... do you know?"

"I'd heard it may have involved Leo Fratn—"

"Leo Fratnik?"

Was there anyone in this town who didn't know Leo? It would appear not.

"It's just what I heard," I said.

"Oh, *come on*. You're being ridiculous. Whoever suggested anything went on between the two of them is a liar."

Perhaps.

"I asked Leo," I said. "He denied it."

"Of course he did because it's not true. I can't believe you asked him at all. I can imagine how pissed he must have been when you accused him."

I shrugged. "I like to get to the point."

"Yes ... I can see you do."

There were a couple of ticks of silence as we sized each other up. I could almost hear the wheels churning in Maria's head, though I was unclear about what she was focusing on right now.

Was she angry because I'd spoken ill of the dead?

Or was she angry because the rumor was, in fact, fact, and I'd found out about it?

Was it possible she knew something she wasn't saying?

She traced circles on the table with her finger and then huffed a quiet, "I'm sorry."

I leaned forward.

"Sorry?"

More ticks of silence. A feather-like touch of dread rushed through me.

I pushed harder.

"Maria, *why* are you sorry?"

She looked over at me, and tears streamed down her cheeks once more. "I wish I had some information to give you. Some way to help you find Ginny's killer. I loved her. She was my ..."

She choked on a sob, and I grabbed a box of tissues off the counter.

"Here," I said, handing them over to her. "Now *I'm* sorry. I didn't mean to upset you."

She wiped her eyes, blew her nose, and looked up at me. "I don't think you understand. When I say I loved her, I mean ... I *really* loved her."

Ding, ding.

The lightbulb went on.

"Oh, I see."

28

"I knew there was no chance for us, her being married and all," Maria said. "And then Diego died, and I had a glimmer of hope. I thought maybe, after some time passed ..."

Oh. My. Stars.

I did my best to restrain the absolute shock I was feeling.

Start with the basics, Sloane.

Nice and slow.

"Was Ginny aware of how you felt?" I asked.

Maria bit her lip, nodded.

I dreaded my next question, but it had to be asked. "Did she feel the same way?"

She shook her head. "No. She did not."

My heart raced, my mind working overtime.

I took in a slow breath and released it.

Had the sting of Ginny's rejection been too much for Maria to take?

Was I sitting across from Ginny's killer?

"Where were you last Thursday?" I asked.

Her eyes widened. "Are you serious? I just pour my heart out to you, a complete stranger, and now you think *I* killed her?"

"I'm not accusing you of anything. I need to look at all the possibilities. You understand, don't you?"

"I don't," she snapped. "Get the hell out of my house."

I ignored the command and continued. "This can all be cleared up if you tell me where you were on Thursday."

"I don't have to talk to you."

"No, but you *will* have to talk to someone. Me or the cops. If not me, let's start with the cops." I stood. "You're right. I should be going. I have a phone call to make."

"Sloane ... hold on."

I crossed my arms and tapped my shoe on the ground, waiting.

"I was here Thursday, okay? Tommy was with me."

The perfect alibi.

Tommy was far too young to remember the exact day or time he was at the house with his mom.

"And my father came to visit," she added. "He stayed for a few days. That's why Louie and Tommy haven't played together much lately."

"And you're telling me you didn't know Ginny was missing."

She reached for another tissue and said, "Right. I had no idea ... until now."

My bullshit radar was bouncing between innocence and guilt. Part of me wanted to believe her. The other part didn't.

"The police will be in touch, Maria," I said. "I hope you're telling the truth, because if Louie has to deal with one more piece of bad news ... if we have to tell him his friend's mother ..."

I threw my hands in the air, too irritated to finish. I called for Louie to come downstairs and left her sniveling into her box of tissues.

29

When Maddie and I had some downtime that evening, I shared the details of what Lisa's mom had told me, Leo's denial, then Maria's revelation.

Maddie paced the floor, her damp braid swinging from side to side. "I don't know how many more surprises I can take."

I felt the same way. "Now that I've told you, I need to tell Flint."

She stopped pacing and looked me in the eye. "Do you think it's possible? Do you think Maria killed Ginny?"

I shrugged. "Some of her reactions seemed a bit strange when I think about it. I guess she could have, yes. Then again, I could go the other way. She seemed broken up when I gave her the news about Ginny's death."

"Not all killers are easy to read. Where's Tommy's dad? Maybe we need to talk to him too."

Good question.

"You know, I got so caught up in the conversation about Maria's crush on Ginny, I never asked if she was married, separated, or what. It won't take long for Flint to figure out. I just hope at the end of all this, Louie doesn't lose Tommy. He needs all the friends he can get right now."

"If she's innocent, it shouldn't make one bit of difference."

I nodded. "And if she's not ..."

"If she's not, it's not Tommy's fault."

She was right, but would Louie see it that way?

Maddie splayed herself across the chair next to the couch, her arm over her eyes. "Ugh. I don't want to think about this anymore tonight. I can't. I need to find a pause button somewhere and press it."

Message received.

We were all in need of comfort food.

"What do you want to do for dinner?" I asked.

"Nothing, I'm not hungry. I don't think I could eat."

"How about one of those big Greek salads and some pizza?"

She peeked out from under her arm.

I had her attention.

"You relax," I said. "I'll place the order and then get in touch with Flint to fill him in."

I ordered dinner and then called the detective. When I told him about the "affair" angle, he responded with a simple, "We'll check it out." Then, in a gentle way, he suggested I butt out. Again.

At this point, I was used to hearing it.

And he was used to understanding it wouldn't make a bit of difference.

On my way to pick up dinner, I decided to stop in and see Nick. I'd called the hospital beforehand and confirmed I had just enough time to chat with him before visiting hours were over. I also called Tara. I asked if she was holding up okay and whether or not she was with Nick. She wasn't, which was perfect. I wanted a few minutes alone with him.

I arrived at the hospital and found Nick sitting up in bed with the remnants of a meal on the tray in front of him.

"Wow, this is a surprise," he said with a grin. "Great to see you again."

"Great to see you alive and well. You gave everyone a scare."

He pushed the tray away and rubbed his forehead. "I'll admit it was scary ... and just so bizarre."

"Yeah, Tara mentioned something about you feeling dizzy right before the accident happened. What do you remember?"

He shifted in bed so he could sit up straighter. "Not much. I just remember feeling, like, wavy."

"Wavy?" I said, smiling. "Interesting way to put it."

He laughed. "I know, but that's what comes to mind. I couldn't focus or think straight."

"What do the doctors say?"

"They blame it on the heat. They don't think it's anything to worry about."

"What do *you* think?"

"Me? I think it's damn strange. I've never had trouble in the heat before. Hell, I work in hotter conditions most days."

"Maybe a medication you're taking could have caused it?"

"I don't take any meds. And I don't do drugs." His expression was earnest, and I found myself believing him.

"Not much alcohol beforehand, right?"

"I'd just finished a beer when we went out. My first of the day."

I pulled up the one chair in the room, sat down, and leaned forward, making direct eye contact. "The beer came from where?"

He narrowed his gaze. "What are you asking?"

"Just wondering if you could have been drugged. Someone slipped something into your drink maybe."

He burst out laughing.

But I wasn't kidding.

"I'm not kidding," I said.

He blinked at me and said, "What's with all the suspicion?"

"I'm a PI, Nick. It's my nature." I leaned back. "It just seems odd that this would have happened to you, those symptoms. You're lucky, I guess, that you didn't hit more than the rope."

"What—you think someone's trying to kill me?" He snorted out a laugh.

I shrugged. Opportunity to prove Nick had been—or had not been—mickeyed was long gone now. I wished I'd thought to grab the beer can or bottle he'd been sipping from. Of course, so much had changed between then and now. I wouldn't have thought of it then. But if it had happened today ...

I changed subjects. "I guess Tara has told you about Ginny by now, huh?"

"She did." His expression turned somber, and he swallowed hard. "It's sad. So much tragedy for one family. Too much."

I agreed.

"How's Tara doing?"

"Not well. First my accident, then the news of Ginny's death. She's been crying for days. When I get out of here, I'm taking her away from all this—somewhere she can relax and unwind."

Good plan.

I hoped to do the same with Maddie.

I checked the time and then stood. "I'm glad you're feeling better."

"Hey, before you go, what are the cops saying about Ginny's murder? Do they have any leads?"

"More leads than you would think." I thought about my conversation with Maria a few hours before, a conversation I wasn't ready to share with anyone else at this point. "Seems Leo knows something—"

"I heard he'd been brought in for questioning, then released."

"True. I think he made a deal for information leading to Ginny's whereabouts and maybe even her killer, but Detective Flint isn't saying much."

"Hmm."

"You don't happen to know if Ginny was involved with someone since Diego's death, do you? Or maybe even while he was alive? In a romantic way, I mean."

His eyes widened. "That's crazy talk right there."

"How so? Affairs happen all the time."

"I suppose they do," he said with a sigh. "Ginny was distracted, nervous even, after Diego's death. I figured it was due to the stress she felt over losing her husband, but I guess it could have been something else."

I latched on to his comment. "You're right. It could have been stress related or it could have been something more. What if she found out something, ahh, sketchy, let's say? Or even illegal, and was about to blow the whistle?"

"Damn, being suspicious *is* second nature to you, isn't it? Well, I can say this. If there was something illegal or otherwise going on in her world, Ginny wouldn't have stopped until the bad guys were caught."

I patted his leg and said, "Except if she was dead."

Nick stared at me for a minute and then said, "You're right. Holy ... shit."

30

I spared Maddie any discussion of "murder" and "murder suspects" and instead snuggled in with her on the couch after putting Louie to bed. I didn't even tell her I'd gone to see Nick before picking up dinner. All in due time, which wasn't now.

She watched TV, and I pretended to watch TV. Or maybe she was pretending too. But we just stayed like that for several hours, silent. Watching. Waiting.

When morning rolled around, I considered my next steps. I could talk to Dom Andino, see if he had any thoughts on Nick's near-fatal accident. I buzzed Nick in the hospital to snag Dom's number, pleased when he gave it to me.

"He just left, in fact," Nick said. "I'm sure he'd be happy to talk to you, but I don't know what else he could tell you."

Few people were happy to talk to me when I was in this mode—detective mode—but I didn't have to share that with Nick. I thanked him and dialed the Adonis.

Dom and I agreed to meet at a café in the bustling downtown area, and Maddie took Louie to Fred Howard Park where he could blow off some steam running around with Charlie.

I took an Uber to the place Dom suggested we meet—a

café behind an old train station that had been turned into a historical museum. I found Dom seated outside, shoveling in a huge salad. He wore a loose white tank and black spandex leggings.

"Yo, Sloane," he said between bites. "Have a sit." He pointed to the obvious chair on the other side of the small table. I followed the line of his arm all the way down to his hand, a wave of muscles rippling toward the fingertips.

Maybe I should have let Maddie do this drill instead.

I took a seat and tried to focus anywhere there weren't muscles popping out, which wasn't easy.

"Thanks for seeing me," I said.

"Not a problem. You want anything?"

"I'm good."

He looked up and summoned a waiter who had just come outside to deliver food to another table. "Can we get a water for the lady, please?"

So much for listening, though the water was a nice gesture.

Once it had been delivered to the table, I said, "I wanted to ask what you remember about Nick's accident."

He shrugged, took a bite of salad, chewed. "Why? It was just an accident. Besides, he's fine."

"Nothing unusual happened just before he went out on the jet ski?"

"Unusual like what?"

"Drugs, alcohol, an argument with someone ... I don't know."

He shook his head and scrunched up his perfect Grecian nose. "Nah. Nothing like that. He scared the shit out of me though. I love him like he's my own brother."

I remembered how upset Dom had seemed when making the emergency call. Could it have been an act? Was he acting now? Or was he telling me the truth?

I didn't know why my hackles were up about Nick's accident, but they were. I thought about it some more and realized I *did* know why I was pursuing this line of thinking:

Because of what I'd seen in the back room at Leo's tavern, and ...

Because Nick's name was on the paperwork I'd seen, and ...

Because he'd become so dizzy on the jet ski he'd almost killed himself, and ...

Because Dom had insisted that Nick go to his boat instead of staying with our group.

And who were the other men on Dom's boat?

I thought about the guy with the huge snake-and-dagger tattoo on his arm, his eyes as flat and cold as the inked snake.

"The other people on the boat that day ... can I get their names and contact info?" I asked.

He quirked an eyebrow, set his fork on his plate, and leaned back in his chair. "Look, it was a terrible thing, what happened to Nicky. But there's nothing weird going on. It was just one of those things."

"Yeah, seems everyone feels the same way."

He picked up his fork and pointed it at me. "Everyone except *you*."

I smiled. "What about those names then?"

"Not gonna happen, sweets. Sorry."

"Thanks for your time, Dom." I stood and headed out of the café, feeling his eyes on me the whole way.

Like snake eyes.

The conversation had reaped the worst possible outcome.

Zip. Zero. Nada.

31

All the way back to the house, the whole whodunit conundrum took up full space in my brain. I could think of nothing else.

Was I becoming obsessed?

Damn right I was.

I still was getting no straight answers from anyone. So be it. That didn't mean the answers weren't attainable by other means.

I pulled into the driveway with Ginny's murder on my mind. She had known something, and it had gotten her killed—I now believed that for sure. It wasn't a lover's squabble or that she'd stepped in front of a speeding bullet by accident. It was something else—something I did not yet understand.

In fact, "accident" was what had the blood zipping through my veins.

Too many damn accidents in this quaint little town.

Ginny had been jumpy, nervous since the death of her husband—several people had said so. Was it her way of grieving, or was she worried about something, someone? I was leaning toward the latter.

I recalled Nick's words about Ginny: *"If there was something illegal or otherwise going on in her world, Ginny wouldn't have stopped until the bad guys were caught."*

She had known something, and she'd been killed because of it.

I thought of the insurance papers and the photos in the back room at the tavern.

Leo had given the police information in exchange for a more lenient deal for himself. Whatever that was, I didn't know and didn't care, but there was a connection there. Ginny's murder, Louie's drawings, the accidents, the associated players, and what I'd discovered at the tavern. Ginny being all wound up prior to her death. But why?

A tingle crept up my spine and had me shivering as I stepped inside the house.

Who would be next to have an accident?

Time to take another stab at Ginny's office.

I threw my purse on the couch and made a beeline for that room, even though I had to pee in a bad way. It could wait.

No ... it couldn't.

I made a quick detour to the bathroom, gave myself an encouraging look in the mirror—*you're a damn good PI, you will figure this out* —then I headed into Ginny's office.

This time I would get far more personal with my search. Check inside every crevice, every notebook, every file ...

And what about her computer?

Could I log into her computer?

I could not. It was password protected. I tried a few random ideas, none of which scored me a win.

I was not deterred. I opened the filing cabinet and perused everything—all the artwork by Louie, every legal document, every birthday card. Heck, I even riffled through a bunch of user manuals for appliances and most of the books on the shelves. Nothing jumped out.

I was not deterred. I lifted the area rug, stuffed my hand between cushions, lifted the desk lamp, the printer, the garbage can.

I went back and sat in the swivel chair and opened the desk

drawers. Last time, I'd just shuffled through them. Now I took out every single item. Every paperclip, every pen, every notebook.

There were three spiral-bound notebooks, like the size of a journal. I opened the first one, and it was nothing but grocery lists and to-do lists. I inspected each one for anything out of the ordinary, but it was all basic stuff. Reminders of a life that had been full, worth living.

I opened the second notebook and started reading, my heart swelling at the love I saw on the pages.

It was a journal shared between husband and wife, their signatures after each entry proof of that. Diego would write one thing on any given day, and Ginny would respond. Back and forth it went, even if it was just a brief sentence or a drawing of a heart with an arrow through it, little legs and eyes added to make it into a person. Sappy stuff. But as Maddie would say: *adorbs.*

How tragic they would both wind up dead …

Wait.

A thought occurred to me, something I should have considered before.

Had Diego been closing in on some illegal scenario and was killed because of it? His death had been made to look like an accident, but what if it was to shut him up? If true, had he shared that knowledge with Ginny, thereby leaving her holding the evidence that would get her killed too?

Dead men told no tales.

I opened the third notebook and realized I was wrong.

Yes, in this case, dead men do.

32

The third notebook contained some telling data. Intriguing data. There had been some "detective-ing" going on within the walls of this home, it seemed. Diego and Ginny had been researching accidental deaths in the local area.

All men.

All married.

All dying in the last year or so.

Theo Watson died March 15. Drowned in rough seas.
John Smitty died February 25. T-boned in a car wreck.
Demetrius Faldo died May 20. Fell and impaled himself on rebar.

There were another six entries, all much of the same with dates in no particular order. And then the most chilling entry of all:

There are many ways to accidentally kill someone.

Based on notebook #2, I could tell the handwriting must have been a mix of both Diego's and Ginny's.

Nine men, dead by accidents in the first half of this year alone. Add to that Diego Alvarez, and we had ten in the local area.

In reading the entries, I could have almost come to the conclusion that Maddie's sister and brother-in-law were the ones who'd done the deeds. Like a murder book, right there in front of me.

Except Diego was dead too.

And now Ginny.

This was the dangerous knowledge I'd been seeking. I took the second and third notebooks with me to the guest room and shoved them into my suitcase, to share at some point in the near future with Flint. Perhaps he was already onto this train of thought and had connected the same dots I just had. I sat on the bed and rubbed my forehead, pulling my eyebrows taut and rolling my eyes back. A weird sort of brain stretch. My mind was blown.

Could it be ...?

Wives were killing their husbands for the insurance money, and someone was getting a cut. Or perhaps these wives were *forced* to participate in the murder-for-money scam—some sort of threat involved to keep them silent.

Either way, it would take many moving parts to pull something like that off.

I gasped as I thought of Nick. I had seen his photo right there on the table in the tavern, alongside the paperwork I'd found.

Was Tara being threatened, forced to allow these people to off her husband and collect on the insurance money?

It was something to consider. Poor Tara. First her friends, and now she may have been right in the same hell loop Ginny had been in. How many more would die before someone stopped the madness?

33

"Sloane-y, we're home-y."

I groaned at the sound of Maddie's voice, knowing it meant I would soon need to deliver another blow to her already fragile mental state. Though maybe she would focus on the positive, and it *was* a positive. Her sister and brother-in-law had been tracking an insurance scam—death for dough—and were close to exposing it.

Until they were silenced.

I rolled off the bed and shuffled down the hall toward the kitchen. My legs felt like cannonballs. This was not a conversation I wanted to have.

Maddie and Louie were leaning against the center island, sipping on some juice boxes. They both had sand all over them—their hair, their feet, their arms. I had the sudden urge to spray them down with a hose.

"What's with all the sand? I thought you were going to a park?"

Maddie shrugged. "Park had sand."

"Ah. Of course, it did."

Charlie scampered out of the laundry room, revealing he had enjoyed the sand-scapade as much as anyone else.

"Don't you think you guys should rinse off—"

"Zip it, sister," Maddie said with a grin. "Any luck with Dom?"

"Not much. I mean, he was nice enough. I wanted the names of his friends on the boat, and he cut me off, ending the conversation at that point."

Maddie shrugged. "I understand, I guess. No need to put everyone under a microscope. It was just an accident, what happened to Nick."

"But what if it wasn't?"

She stared at me, straw stuck between her lips. She pulled the straw away and set the juice box on the countertop. "What in Sam Adams...?"

"I think what you mean to say is, 'What in Sam Hill...'"

She shook her head and groaned. "I don't care about Sam anyone. What are you talking about?"

I looked at Louie and said, "Why don't you and Charlie rinse yourselves off with the hose out back?"

Louie's eyes lit up, and boy and dog made a break for the sliding glass door.

Once they were outside, Maddie wasted no time getting right to the point. "Sloane? Tell me what's going on in that big brain of yours."

And so I did. I showed her the notebooks, told her my theories, and gave her a moment to process before saying, "So what do you think?"

"I *think* you're amazing. I think this is horrible. Even so, it's what we needed to know. We need to contact Flint."

"Of course, yes. I agree. He may have discovered some things already, but even if he has, he doesn't have these notebooks."

"Sloane, this could be the proof ..." She stopped there, holding her throat as emotion took over.

"To nab your sister's killer. Maybe even Diego's killer. I sure hope so, Maddie."

She looked up, terror alit in her eyes. "Oh no."

"Oh no, what?"

"Tara is Ginny's friend. She might know some or all of this information. What if she feels she can't tell anyone? What if she thinks if she did, they, whoever 'they' are, would try to silence her too?"

"I'll admit, I've been wondering the same thing," I said. "For now, let's not freak out. I don't want to share any of this with Tara until we're sure."

"I'm not freaking out."

"Yeah, you are. We don't know if she knows or what she knows yet. We need to call Flint pronto."

"I'm on it," Maddie said.

She placed the call. It wasn't a success. At present, Flint was otherwise engaged. Maddie left a message, and now all we could do was wait.

"Let's give it a half hour or so, then try again," I suggested, though my patience was thinning. While I'd kind of wanted to keep the new info to myself for a little longer—if not for any other reason than because I wanted a little more time to learn about the insurance scam and who else was involved—I was now anxious to hop on that horse and ride into the sunset, white hat and all, case just about solved. All I needed now was the killer.

Maddie glanced toward the back yard and said, "Ahh, I think we should intervene."

Louie and Charlie were running around in circles, Louie spraying Charlie, Charlie trying to bite the hose. And while it was cute and offered us a temporary reprieve from all the heaviness, Maddie was right. The mayhem needed to be reined in.

I stepped outside to offer new marching orders and was walloped straight in the face with a cool blast from the hose. I sputtered and wiped my eyes. Maddie was holding her gut, laughing behind me. Quick as a wink, I grabbed the hose from Louie and doused my best friend from head to toe. She ran around the yard, screaming and trying to escape my water fire.

I heard a jingling of a phone from inside the house.

Maddie and I locked eyes, then ran into the kitchen.

She grabbed the phone and said, "Detective Flint? Have we got news for you."

34

After switching the phone to speaker mode, Maddie placed it on the kitchen table, and we hovered around it. Before I could say a word, Maddie delivered a rambling, untethered version of my recent discovery and our resulting theories. To say she was excited was an understatement.

Once she'd finished, Flint suggested we take a step back and come to the station for a face-to-face meeting. It was dinnertime, and we were starving, but we were both happy to oblige.

"Don't forget to bring the notebooks," he said before we hung up.

As if we needed reminding.

"I should have let you speak to him," Maddie said. "Sorry."

I placed my hand on hers and gave it a squeeze. "Going into the station is what I prefer. In person is better. You can miss so much with a phone call. And who knows? Maybe I'll be able to pick up a few additional clues as to who Flint may be pursuing as the killer right now."

Her shoulders dropped as if they were bearing the weight of the world. I supposed they were. She and her siblings had already been discussing who would take care of Louie now. Even though I hadn't known the little tyke for long, I'd grown attached to him in the short time I'd been there. What would become of him had been weighing on my mind too.

I guessed Detective Flint had been gathering evidence that would be irrefutable before he made any arrests, evidence that would stick in court. Biding his time, he'd been waiting, watching. I hoped the notebooks along with our take on things would be added to whatever evidence he already had, moving the case forward, faster.

Louie and Charlie came in from the back yard, both wet and smelling like they were in desperate need of a shower.

"Okay, boys," I said. "Let's hustle to the bathroom ... the one in your mom's room."

Louie looked surprised.

"It's a bigger bathtub," I said by way of explanation.

I'd seen the elegant bathroom during one of my snoop sessions. The tub alone was the size of an outdoor jacuzzi.

I turned toward Maddie. "I'll supervise bath time. You get on the horn with Lynn. See if she can watch Louie while we go to the station."

After a half hour of total shower mayhem, I had both boys dried off and Louie dressed in a fresh pair of shorts and a t-shirt. I, on the other hand, needed a shower of my own. Flint may have been waiting for us, but it had to be done.

Maddie stepped into the hall just as I was coming out of the guestroom with a fresh set of clothes in hand.

"My turn for a shower," I said.

"Yeah, you, ehh ... need one. I've never seen your hair so ..." She held her hands up like they were claws. "You have a *rarrrhh*, wild tigress look going."

I shook my head at her and proceeded into the bathroom.

"Hey, Lynn will be here in fifteen minutes," she said.

Fifteen minutes was all I needed.

"Perfect," I said. "Louie's in his room. He's exhausted. He may have even fallen asleep."

"I'll let him know Lynn's coming."

"Great. I'll be out in a flash."

And I was.

Lynn arrived and greeted Louie with a big bear hug. I thanked her for coming on such short notice and then added, "Maddie updated you on everything when she called, right? I know it's a risk, you being here with Louie when his life may be in danger. We won't be long, and if it's too much, we'll take him with us and figure something out. The truth is, we don't trust anyone else with him."

Lynn grinned and patted her hip a few times. "Ladies, I'm armed, and, well ... I'm plenty dangerous. I'm one of the best shots in the state. Placed second in the women's shooting competition last month. Not too shabby. Anyone tries to get into this house won't leave here alive. I can guarantee you this, no harm will come to that sweet boy."

It was a relief.

During my shower, I'd thought about canceling with Lynn, knowing we wouldn't be able to bear it if something happened to Louie, something we could have prevented.

"Thanks again." I glanced at Maddie. "You ready to go?"

She held the keys up, dangling them on one finger. "Yep, let's get moving."

We made it to the station without further ado and noticed Detective Flint waiting for us at the front door. It was nice to see him so eager. We had something he wanted and needed, for once. I hoped he would return the favor with some intel of his own.

We settled at his desk in the bullpen, and a female officer joined us, pulling up a chair next to Flint.

"This is Detective Kat Smart," he said. "She's been assisting me with this investigation."

"What a great name for a detective," Maddie said.

Smart winked. "Let's hope it helps us find the killer, right?"

I whipped out the notebooks and laid them in front of Flint. I pointed to the notebook with the love notes in it. "I brought this one so you can see the handwriting of both Diego and Ginny. It's important in relation to the next notebook."

Flint and Smart inspected a few pages.

Smart read a few entries and said, "Aww, how sweet."

Flint grunted a "hmm," then opened the other notebook. He flipped through the pages, then went back to the beginning and flipped through them again. Smart hovered over his shoulder, reading right along with him.

"They were working on this together," Flint said. "Well, I'll be damned."

"Someone's damned, that's for sure," I said.

I explained my thoughts about the murders based on what I'd discovered in the notebooks, looping back to some of the conversations I'd had with pertinent parties ever since the day Ginny went missing. I updated him on my non-conversation with Dom as well.

"I know Dom," Smart said.

The way she'd said it made me think he was more than an acquaintance. The look on her face reminded me of the way I felt about some of my exes. Perhaps the two had been an item.

"I take it you don't like Dom," I said. "Seems like a nice enough guy to me."

I looked at Maddie, who nodded in agreement.

"He's a charmer, all right," Smart said, giving Flint the side-eye.

Flint noticed and said, "Go ahead and tell them. Trust me ... *this* one"—he pointed at me—"won't let it rest until you explain yourself."

He said it with a grin, but he was spot-on. I wouldn't let it rest. Up to now, I'd had vague suspicions surrounding Dom but nothing I could sink my teeth into. If there was something she knew and I didn't, I needed to know.

Smart sat back in her chair, stretched her arms over her head, and said, "Okay, so we used to date. In fact, we were serious at one point, like official boyfriend/girlfriend status. I thought he might be the one, you know? He was gorgeous, funny, took good care of himself. Heck, he took good care of me."

It didn't surprise me. Smart was easy on the eyes, with pitch-black hair in an angled bob and brown eyes so dark the pupil was barely visible. Deep chocolate pools. She was slender but toned, her slacks and short-sleeved blouse showing off muscles and curves in all the right places. But the thing I was drawn to most was her matter-of-fact way of communicating and how she carried herself. It was obvious she didn't allow anyone to mess with her.

"You say he took good care of you," I said. "In what way?"

"He was understanding about my job. He was always there for me. He bought me countless gifts, reminded me how much he loved me."

"I sense a *but* coming," Maddie said.

Smart nodded. "He was a con artist. A drug dealer. Roid brain to boot, though he never got violent with me."

"And you knew this about him ... how, when?" I asked.

"I didn't know about it at all while we were dating. I found out by accident, during a sting operation we conducted earlier this year. I ended up arresting him myself. And you wanna know something? I didn't shed one damn tear when I did it."

35

Before leaving the station, Detective Flint asked us to lie low when it came to revealing anything about the notebooks or our theories to anyone. We'd made the promise, something easy enough to do. Neither of us wanted to impede the investigation or cause anyone else to be hurt. This was one of those times when I was okay with letting the police take over. For a red-hot minute, anyway. It didn't mean I wouldn't stew about it or drive myself crazy thinking about it, waiting for them to nab whoever was on their radar.

I drove us back to the house, and it was a silent ride. It seemed we were both soaking in the implications of what Detective Smart had shared with us. I'd driven to the station hoping Flint would offer up some intriguing information for once. Imagine my surprise when it had come from his partner on the case instead.

Maddie's phone rang, and she put it on speaker. "Hey, Tara. How's it going?"

"Not bad. How are you two?"

"We've been better," Maddie said. "Oh, Tara. You won't believe what we discovered."

I poked Maddie in the shoulder and did a "knife across the throat" gesture. Had she already forgotten what Detective Flint had said about not talking to *anyone* about the information we'd just handed over?

After a long pause wherein Maddie didn't seem to know what to say to recover, Tara said, "Well, what did you find out? Something about Ginny's murder?"

"We found out ... that ... ahh ... Charlie loves being chased with a hose!" Maddie began laughing a bit too hard and then continued the charade adding, "You should have seen it, Tara. He thought the hose was a snake or something, kept trying to bite it. And Louie just kept spraying him."

Maddie looked at me and said, "It was hilarious wasn't it, Sloane?"

"Ha!" It was the best I could do in the moment. "Maddie's right. It was so cute."

Tara went silent, and I wondered whether she'd bought the story we were selling. Then she said, "Listen, I bought Louie a new Nerf gun while I was at the store today, and I'd like to stop by and give it to him if it's okay with you."

"We're not at the house right now," Maddie said.

"Oh? What are you guys up to tonight?"

"We're ahh ... we just stepped out to get some groceries," Maddie said.

Good save.

"How long until you guys get home?" Tara asked.

"Maybe twenty minutes?" Maddie said.

"Great," Tara said. "See you then."

Before we had the chance to suggest she come tomorrow, the line went dead. I frowned at Maddie.

"What?" she said. "I thought I handled it all right. Didn't I?"

I jerked the wheel and did a one-eighty, headed back in the direction we'd just come from.

Maddie looked confused.

"Groceries, remember?" I said. "We can't walk in empty-handed now."

"Right. Oops. I guess I messed up."

"Hey, you did great. I'm sorry. We're both a bit on edge tonight. Speaking of being on edge … I've been thinking. Do you think it's possible Dom was the reason Nick almost got his head chopped off at the beach the other day?"

"Why? Because he's a druggie?" She shrugged. "Who knows?"

"For a while, I've been thinking Nick may have been drugged before he got on the jet ski. I'd gone to see Nick in the hospital and—"

"Wait. What? When?"

"Before I picked up dinner yesterday. Doesn't matter. Point is, I asked him if he thought he might have been drugged. I figured it would explain the reason for his sudden dizziness on the watercraft and his subsequent eating of the anchor line. Of course, he nixed the idea at first, but after we talked about it some more, I felt like he at least considered it as a possibility."

"Nick would know about Dom's drug-related arrest. They're close friends since, like, forever," Maddie said.

"Do you think Nick's involved in drugs of any kind?"

She shook her head. "No, I don't. Ginny would never have allowed him near her home if she knew he had a drug problem."

I considered her response and decided to take her word for it. I didn't need another rabbit hole to venture into. But Dom on the other hand …

"Dom could have done it," I said. "Or maybe one of the other guys on the boat. Maybe they're the people causing all of these 'accidental' deaths."

She turned to stare at me, her eyes bugged out. I noticed her jaw was twitching, and she was gritting her teeth.

Was she angry?

About to cry?

"You wanna know something?" she said. "This whole thing. People killing each other for money. It's just, I'm so pissed."

"I know. It's a lot to take in."

I turned into the parking lot of a Publix supermarket, and we made quick work of it, speeding down the aisles, selecting food we imagined Louie would like, nutritious or otherwise. We also made sure to buy a few bottles of wine for self-medication. At this point, we both needed it. We paid for the food, grabbed the bags, and loaded up the car.

We pulled into the driveway several minutes later, and Louie came running out to greet us. Lynn followed close behind. We thanked her, gifted her one of the bottles of wine we'd bought, and she left for home.

I breathed a sigh of relief. "I wasn't sure we'd make it back before Tara—" Just as the words left my lips, Tara's car turned onto our street. She parked in the driveway and got out, the bangles on her arms jingling as she made her way toward us. Tonight, her hair was styled into a high ponytail. In one hand, she held a wrapped gift. I assumed it was the Nerf gun she'd bought Louie. She glanced at the three grocery bags in the trunk like she wondered why we hadn't bought more, and said, "I have a free hand. Let me help with those."

I handed her a bag, and she peeked inside. "Ooh, wine. I could use a glass."

"I think we all could," I said.

Tara nodded and headed into the house. Just as she reached the threshold, she called over her shoulder, "By the way ... how'd it go at the police station?"

36

I stood there, stunned, wondering how in the hell Tara had known where we'd gone. I hated when shit like that happened. Here we thought we'd pulled the wool over her eyes, and we hadn't. Somehow, she'd found out. What's more, she seemed hellbent on making sure we knew she knew about it.

Neither Maddie nor I responded, focusing instead on taking the groceries into the house and putting them away. I then poured three glasses of red wine. Tara gave Louie his gift. He tore open the wrap to reveal the Nerf gun, and his eyes lit up. He grabbed a Lunchable out of the refrigerator and took it and the gun into the living room. I heard the TV go on and the surfing of channels until he'd found the show he wanted to watch.

"Why don't we enjoy our beverages on the patio out back?" Maddie suggested.

We headed outside and sipped in silence for all of thirty seconds before I couldn't take it anymore. I had to know what she knew and what she didn't.

"Tara, why did you ask us where we were going on the phone if you already knew?"

She smirked, looking at me over the rim of her wineglass. "I *didn't* know at first."

"Are you *spying* on us?" Maddie asked, her expression one of complete disbelief. "Why would you—"

Tara interrupted with a wave of her hand and a giggle. "No, no. Nothing like that. After our conversation ended, one of my friends called. She said she saw Sloane going into the police station."

"Why would anyone take note of me? I've never even been here before."

"You met her at the tavern when you were asking questions. She's one of the waitresses."

"Ahh. Which one?"

"Melissa Walker. Super cute, super tall, spiky blond hair, remember?"

I nodded. "Right. She had nothing helpful to share with me when I questioned her." My spidey senses started tingling. Something wasn't right. Why would this woman be reporting on my activities? "So, is that the reason she called you? Because she saw me at the station?"

"Seems a bit weird, Tara," Maddie chimed in.

Tara held up her hands. "Ladies, chill please. She's a friend of mine, and we were planning a time to get together. She happened to be taking the restaurant deposit to the bank before it closed and saw you two entering the police station. She made a simple mention of it. It was no big deal."

Seemed like a valid explanation. For now.

"Sorry," I said. "We're just on edge."

"Why *were you* at the station? Have they found Ginny's killer yet?" Tara stared down at her hands, wiping a tear from her eye. "It's all I've been able to think about since I learned she was murdered."

Maddie started to speak, and I jumped in, just to be on the safe side. "We can't go into detail about the conversation we had at the station. Detective Flint had some questions. We stopped in, answered them, and he asked us to keep the conversation to ourselves for now."

"But I'm like family," Tara said, looking put out by the fact she wasn't included in the latest scoop. If only she knew—or maybe she did—it was for her own welfare.

"Maybe I should talk to Melissa Walker again," I said. "Last time, she seemed too preoccupied to discuss what she knew about Ginny. That was before any of us knew Ginny was murdered. I can't help but wonder if she's remembered something more about the day Ginny went missing."

"What makes you think she would?" Tara asked.

"I just ... I don't know. I guess I find it odd that she took the time to mention she'd seen me at the police station. Maybe she knows something she hasn't said."

"If she did, I'm sure she would have told me. I think talking to her again would be a waste of your time."

Now my hackles were up.

Who was she to say what was a waste of my time and what wasn't?

"Perhaps you're right." I leaned back, took a sip of wine. "It's been a long day, and I'm wiped out. What about you, Maddie?"

Maddie nodded. "Sorry, Tara. We're going to turn in."

Tara stood and drained her glass. "No problem. Thanks for letting me come over. Seeing Louie and his sweet face is keeping me from having a complete meltdown. I'll go give him a quick squeeze and head home."

And then I'd go have another chat with Melissa Walker.

37

It was possible Melissa wouldn't have anything new to say, but something about Tara insisting I not speak with her bugged me. I placed a quick call to the restaurant and learned Melissa was working the evening shift. Perfect. On my way out the door, Maddie made me promise to call her the minute I arrived and the minute I left the restaurant.

I promised.

When I pulled up to the restaurant and parked, I texted Maddie: *I'm here.*

She texted back: *How do I know this is Sloane? ;)*

Even in the most serious of times, she excelled at making things funny.

I gave her a quick call. "It's me, you weirdo. I'll text you again in a bit."

I spotted Melissa leaning against a wall outside of the tavern, smoking a cigarette. Great timing.

I shoved the phone into the back pocket of my denim shorts and headed in Melissa's direction. Then an idea hit me. I took my phone out, set it to record, then slid it into my front pocket.

She smiled as I drew near. "Sloane, right? I was just talking about you."

"Yes, I heard."

She took a drag on her smoke and tilted her head, staring at me. "Oh? What did you hear?"

"Tara stopped by the house tonight to see Louie. While she was there, she told me you'd called her to talk about getting together sometime."

She quirked an eyebrow, looking confused, but didn't say anything.

I continued. "She said you were driving by the police station and saw Maddie and I going inside. I thought I'd stop by again to see if you remembered something more about the day Ginny went missing. Just taking a shot in the dark here."

She stomped out her cigarette with her purple sneaker. "Huh. Well, part of what Tara told you is true."

I raised a brow. "Which part?"

She began to enumerate her points with her fingers. "One, I didn't call her; she called me. Two, we did talk about getting together sometime soon, though I'm not so sure we will. We used to be good friends, but not so much anymore. Three, I've been right here, working for the last several hours. I didn't drive by the police station today at all, in fact. Four, Tara was the one who told me you were at the police station." She paused, as if she were giving me a minute to soak that in. Then she added, "So, either you're lying or she's lying. Which is it?"

I stood there, mouth agape, thinking, *What the hell just happened here?* I rubbed my forehead and tucked my hair behind my ears. "Wow, okay. I wasn't expecting you to say what you just said."

"I take it Tara lied," Melissa deadpanned.

"She sure did. Any idea why?"

"My guess? She just can't help herself. Diversion, lying, being an awkward person to hang out with ... all seem to be second nature to her these past several months." She took out a pack of cigarettes and a lighter from the little handbag—a sequined fish—she had slung over her shoulder. She shook out a smoke then offered the pack to me. "Want one?"

I frowned and shook my head. "No, thank you."

Melissa grinned. "I get it. It's a nasty habit."

Although the sun had gone down, I was still perspiring through my clothes, and my head was starting to ache. Melissa had not a bead of sweat showing anywhere. I guessed she'd lived here long enough to get acclimated to the heat.

I gestured toward the tavern. "Mind if we talk inside?"

She replaced her cigarette in the pack and nodded. "Sure."

"Is Leo here?" I asked knowing if he was, he'd do everything he could to cause my budding headache to fully blossom.

"Nope," she said. "He left a couple of hours ago."

We walked inside and found a table in the corner. I was still a little off-kilter with Melissa's revelation about Tara, so I decided to start with the question I'd intended to ask in the first place.

"Do you happen to remember anything unusual about the day Ginny went missing? Or even something that wasn't unusual at the time, but in retrospect, might seem strange?" I held up a finger. "Oh, and I should add that Tara did not want me to come and talk to you. Do you think she might be guilty of something?"

"Nah, I don't think she's guilty of anything. Ever since Diego's death, she hasn't been the nicest person to be around. I don't dwell on it though. Everyone grieves in their own way. I figured his death hit her hard. They were good friends. And now she's lost Ginny too, which makes it even harder. I'm sure that's why she reached out to me tonight. I'm guessing she needs to vent. I don't blame her. I just don't think I'm the right person. She needs to see a therapist."

"The last time we met, you told me you were working the same shift as Ginny the day she went missing."

"We worked the same shift, yes. The early shift. We both finished about the same time. Tara had dropped Louie off to wait for his mom to take him home. She had an errand to run of some sort and couldn't bring Louie with her."

"Walk through those next minutes with me. Stream-of-consciousness stuff. Whatever you can think of, just say it whether you think it's helpful or not."

She thought about it for a minute. "Okay, so I said hello to Louie, goodbye to Tara, then looked around for Ginny. She wasn't in the main dining area or in the kitchen, so I asked Andy, the bartender, if he knew where she was. He said she was in the back with Leo, which meant either Leo's office or the conference room. I gave Louie an orange soda and some crackers and went to look for Ginny."

"Did you find her?"

"No, I never did, though I didn't look as hard as I could have, to be honest. Someone called for me, and I got sidetracked."

The pained expression on her face matched the pain in my heart. "So, Ginny was somewhere in the restaurant with Leo at some point before Tara arrived with Louie."

"Seems so."

"Are you sure Tara left after she dropped Louie off?"

"She did. I saw her get into her car."

"Did you see her drive away?"

"I wasn't inspecting her every move. But why wouldn't she have? It was clear she was in a hurry to get to wherever she needed to go. And she's not a big fan of Leo. Then again, who is?"

I sighed. "All right. Well, thank you for taking the time to talk to me. It gives me a better picture of that day, at least."

"Wish I was more help. I'm sorry. One minute Ginny was there, talking to me about our shift the following day, and the next—" She stopped talking, her eyes the size of silver dollar.

"What?" I reached out and touched her arm. "What do you remember?"

"You know ... I may have heard something. This place is so noisy,

I didn't think much of it at the time. But now I ... I think what I heard could have been a gunshot. Looking back on the timing and knowing Ginny had been shot when her body was found, now I think—" She stopped short and covered her mouth with her hand.

"It's okay," I said. "Whatever it is. You can say it."

She paused and pressed her hands to her face. "What if *this* is where Ginny died? She was shot, right? Who's to say she wasn't shot at the tavern? I was right here. And no one, none of us, knew better. None of us did anything to help."

She was breaking down, and I didn't blame her. Whether true or not, what a horrible thing to have realized. I didn't want to push her more—but there was one thing I still needed to ask. "When you heard what may have been a gun being fired, where was Louie?"

She shook her head, tears pouring down her cheeks. "I don't know. He was gone."

38

I was back at the house, having driven home in a zombie-like state. My suspicions about that day had been confirmed. I was sure Ginny had been murdered right there at work, with no one the wiser. Except for Louie, who had made a break for it, only to be followed by Frank, who must have also been there when Ginny was shot. Maybe he'd pulled the trigger, even. Who else could have been in that room? Frank, Leo, Dom, Nick ... Tara? I assumed Detective Flint knew most of this, but even if he did, he didn't know about Melissa's newest revelation.

My biggest concern now was for Louie and the danger he was in. The bad guys had seen his face; Frank had been chasing him. When would he, or someone else from that room, return to make sure Louie never, ever spoke about what he'd seen again?

I entered the house and could hear Louie and Maddie in the kitchen. From the sounds of things, they were doing some sort of arts-and-crafts project. I heard the words "glue," "glitter," and "stickers." I was sure Louie was having a ball, given his gift of creativity that he'd exhibited in his artwork.

I paced the living room, my head a jumble of worries and theories. How was I ever going to connect the dots? For the first time, I had to agree with Leo on one thing he'd said. The answer *was* close, right in front of my nose. Information overload was keeping me from seeing the big picture. "I can't see the forest. All I see are trees," I muttered.

I needed to get rid of those trees, and I needed to do it now.

I heard a gasp and spun around. It was Maddie.

"You didn't call me!" she shouted. "I was starting to worry."

"I'm sorry. Everything's all right. I'm safe. But I think we need to get Louie out of this area until the detectives arrest someone for all of the recent murders."

"Melissa remembered something," she whispered, "didn't she?"

I nodded. She sat down, and I told her the horrible truth, something we'd suspected but had not yet been able to confirm without a doubt. "I recorded our conversation."

And I needed to share it with Detectives Flint and Smart.

"Does your sister own a gun?" I asked.

She nodded. "It's in a shoebox at the top of her closet. Wait. You're not ... leaving again, right?"

Not a chance.

"You grab your sister's gun for me. I'll double check all the doors and windows. Then I'll call Detectives Flint and Smart and ask them to come over. When they do, you take Louie into his room and put him to bed while we're talking. Then we'll figure out the next steps we need to take."

I went through the house, ensuring it was locked up tight, and wondering if anyone was out there right now, on the street—watching and waiting for the perfect time to strike. I grabbed my phone and called the police station. When reception answered, I said, "I need to speak with Detective Flint, please. It's urgent. I have information he needs to hear about Ginny Alvarez."

In a lackadaisical, monotone voice, the receptionist said, "One moment please."

Detective Smart came on the line and said, "Sloane? This you? Flint's gone home for the night, but I'm all ears. What's up?"

I gave her a brief overview of the evening, and twenty minutes later, Detective Smart pulled into the driveway. Maddie nodded at me, grabbed Louie's hand, and ushered him to bed. I invited the detective inside, and we convened in the living room.

"All right," she said. "You mentioned something about a recording?"

My phone was on the coffee table in front of us. I hit play for the recording to start. "I haven't even listened to it yet. Might be hard to hear. Don't know how much was caught. I'm hoping it's enough for you to hear—"

"Sloane, take a breath and relax. Let's just listen right now, okay?"

We ran through the entire recording. Some parts were clear; others weren't. But overall, it was clear enough—all the way through to the end.

Luck had been on my side with Melissa Walker.

Smart sat back and clasped her hands over her stomach, twiddled her thumbs. "You shouldn't have gone there, you know. You promised to back off, not say a word."

"I didn't say a word about anything. I just let her talk. You heard it yourself."

She sighed.

"I couldn't *not* go," I continued. "As I explained to you on the phone, Tara had challenged me on that point, and I couldn't stop wondering why she didn't want me to talk to Melissa."

"Could have been for the exact reason Melissa had said—about the change in Tara's behavior after Diego Alvarez died. Maybe Tara didn't want Melissa sharing that information with you; maybe she was embarrassed."

"Do you know Tara?" I asked.

"I know of her, yes."

"So you think she lied to save face?"

She jutted out her jaw, which made her look like she was pouting —though I suspected this woman didn't pout about anything. "Not sure what to think, to be honest. But the best part of all this is Melissa remembered hearing what could have been the shot that killed Ginny. Right there in the tavern."

"Right," I said.

"Which we knew already."

"Yes, Flint had hinted as much to me in one of our previous conversations."

"But we didn't know Louie was there at the same time, not until now," she said.

I leaned in close, and she jerked her head back, caught off guard by my sudden movement. "We need to protect him. You've got to find this killer or killers ..."

"We'll get you, Maddie, and Louie placed somewhere safe tomorrow. I agree, we need to protect him, and not just him ... all of you."

While I agreed Louie needed to be whisked away, I had no intention of going anywhere. Still, I appreciated the gesture she'd made on his behalf.

"Thank you." All the emotion I was feeling pooled together, gathering in my throat. I sat there, smoothing out the wrinkles of my shirt, fighting back the tears.

"I'll be on my way," Smart said with a gentle smile. "I'll talk with Flint, and we'll be in touch tomorrow."

"Can I help—"

She cut me off. "You've already done enough, and it's good work, Sloane. We appreciate it. You need to let us finish this."

"And you will, right? You *will* finish it?"

"We will." She stood. "Keep these doors locked and stay alert. I'll get an officer to patrol the street and keep an eye on the house tonight. We'll see you first thing in the morning to get you somewhere safe."

39

After Detective Smart left, I locked the door and leaned against it, taking a moment to steady my breath. I was tired and unnerved, and a headache still brewing.

Brewing.

Tea.

I needed tea.

And Advil.

Stat.

I headed for the kitchen and riffled through the cabinets, checking out Ginny's tea selection. I settled on relaxation tea, brewed it up, and sat on the couch, my thoughts turning to Maddie and Louie. I would keep us safe until tomorrow, until the police ushered the two of them out of harm's way, and then I'd finish what we'd started. I'd made a commitment to my best friend—to catch her sister's killer—and I intended on making sure justice prevailed.

Louie sauntered into the living room and rubbed his eyes. I didn't blame him. It had been a long day and what felt like an even longer night.

"All right, Louie," I said. "You're going on an adventure with Aunt Maddie tomorrow."

He blinked at me—his eyes wide, full of questions I wasn't sure how to answer.

"A couple of nice police officers are going to take you both somewhere safe, just until they catch the bad guys, the people who hurt your mom. Do you understand?"

He nodded. A tough-like nod with his shoulders thrown back and his chin up. *That's my boy.*

Maddie entered the room and reached for Louie's hand. "Let's go and pack up some clothes and a few of your favorite toys. Maybe some stuff for drawing too, huh?"

He nodded again, and they walked down the hall together. Halfway to his room, he stopped and pointed at Charlie, who was following close behind.

"Of course, we'll need to pack for Charlie too," Maddie said. "We can't go anywhere without him, right?"

Another quick nod by Louie, and off they went. I leaned back, trying hard not to fall asleep. But sleep found me whether I wanted it to or not, and a while later, I woke to the blessed fragrance of green tea, ginseng, tangerine, and lemon.

Maddie was standing in front of me. Her hair was twisted into a giant clip at the top of her head, and she was dressed in something I'd never seen her wear before—a ratty, blue, terrycloth robe.

She set the tea I'd made earlier on the coffee table and said, "You fell asleep with this in your hand. I can't believe you didn't spill it all over yourself. Anyway, I figured you'd be up soon, and I reheated it for you. I took the first watch; you get the second."

I sat up, blinking a few times to allow my eyes to adjust. "How long was I out?

"Over two hours."

Two hours?

I couldn't believe it.

I leaned forward, cupping my hands around the tea. "Thanks, I needed this. You're an angel."

She curtsied, holding the sides of the robe out just a bit. "Heaven sent. That's me all right."

"What's with the housecoat you're wearing?" I asked.

"I found it in Ginny's closet, and I couldn't resist putting it on. I gave it to her for her birthday over a decade ago. I can't believe she still has it. In some strange way, it makes me feel close to her." She sniffed the sleeve. "Smells like her too, like the gardenia fragrance she loved so much."

I checked the time, noting it was just past ten. I held up the mug. "It's relaxation tea. That's what it says on the box anyway. Want to join me? I can make you a cup."

"Nope. I'm off to bed. Louie's already asleep."

"You should have woken me."

"I just did."

"To say goodnight to him, I mean."

"I thought it was best to let you rest. We both could use some down time right about now. By the way, before Louie got in bed, he came out and kissed you on the shoulder." Maddie pressed a finger to my arm. "Right there."

"He's such a good kid. Your sister did a great job raising him."

"Yeah, she did." She paused, bit her lip. "So, you coming to bed too, or ...?"

I shook my head. "I'm wide awake now. I'm think I'll hang out here for a while, keep an eye on things."

She grinned. "I know it's, well, selfish of me, but I'd hoped you'd say that. Even with the cop out on the street, I'll feel a lot better knowing you're looking after us too."

She gave me a squeeze and then headed to bed, leaving me to my own devices, which, at the moment, included a whole lot of ... nothing. Seconds ticked by, then minutes, and my brain tossed and turned, wondering what the morning would bring and how much longer it would be before Detectives Flint and Smart made any arrests.

I sauntered into the kitchen to refill my mug with something a lot more caffeinated, and to find something to eat. I settled on an English muffin topped with butter and raspberry jam. I stood there, leaning against the counter, eating it, and trying not to focus on the dirty dishes in the sink. Five minutes later, the mess got the better of me, and I found myself switching on some music, listening to it on low while I rinsed the dishes.

I loaded the dishwasher, wiped down the countertops and tables, and then wiped down the chairs too. I noticed a smudge of something stuck to the tile floor, so I grabbed a broom and a mop, and worked the entire surface until it was spotless.

Another hour had passed, and there were plenty more to go until daylight. I needed to find another way to occupy my time. I thought about the books I'd seen in Ginny's office. Perhaps one of them would pique my interest.

I switched the music off and decided to look in on "the children" on my way to the office.

I tiptoed into Louie's room. He was fast asleep.

I exited his room and entered the next, peering in at Maddie.

She, too, was fast asleep, and snoring.

Satisfied, I headed toward the home office, freezing outside the door when I thought I heard a sound coming from the opposite side.

I stood still, listening.

Had I heard something?

Or was it all in my head?

I lacked the patience required to wait it out until I was certain. I twisted the doorknob and pushed the door open, surprised to see Tara's wide eyes staring at me from the other side of Ginny's desk.

40

"Tara? What are you doing here?" I hissed.

She had a weird look on her face, a strange mixture of anger and the fear from having been caught.

She said nothing, so I asked again. "What are you doing here?"

And how had she gotten in?

So much for the police officer patrolling the street.

She shrugged. "Sorry, I figured you'd all be sleeping, and I didn't want to wake you, so I let myself in."

Let herself in *where*?

If she'd come through the front door, I would have seen her, which meant she hadn't come through the front door. I canvassed the office. Drawers were open, and it was obvious she'd been shuffling through their contents.

"What are you doing in Ginny's office?" I asked.

I knew why she was there, of course.

I just wanted her to sweat out the question.

She hesitated and then said, "I just needed to pick up something I left here."

I walked over and stood in front of the desk. "How about you stop what you're doing and leave? You can come back another time.

Or you can let me know what you're looking for, and *I'll* find it for you—later."

Tara snapped her head to one side and glared at me. "How about I don't do that, and I get what I came for right now? I'm already here. I'll be in and out in a jiffy."

A million things ran through my mind, pieces of the previous week coming together, forming a clear picture in my mind—a picture that started and ended with Tara.

"You may have been Ginny's friend, but this *isn't* your house," I said. "You're breaking and entering."

She shrugged. "No, I'm not. I have a key. It's no big deal. Like I said before, I didn't want to wake anyone, so I—"

"Maybe you didn't want to wake anyone, or maybe you didn't want to get caught."

I leaned forward.

She leaned back.

I stabbed a finger in her direction. "Get out. I won't ask you again."

"I won't, not until I take what's mine."

We stood there, staring each other down, neither of us relenting.

I gripped my cell phone in my hand, prepared to make a call she wouldn't want me to make.

"You know what? You're a jerk," she said. "Fine. I'm leaving."

No, you're not. Not anymore.

I made a beeline for the door and stood there, crossing my arms.

"Tell me what you know," I demanded. "Tell me what happened to Ginny."

She flailed her arms in frustration, bangles jangling—not a good accessory choice for someone snooping around another person's house.

She faked a smile and attempted to smooth things over by saying, "Look. Ginny was working on something, uh, for me. Doing research. I just need to get those—"

"Notebooks?" I said. "They're what you came for tonight, right?"

Eyes wide, she said, "You've read them?"

"I have. And guess what? They're not here."

"What the hell are you ... What do you mean? Where are they?"

"They're in the hands of the police. I handed them over tonight when you were spying on us—remember? What I'm dying to know is, what do the notebooks have to do with you, Tara?"

"I—" She gazed around the room as if contemplating her next move. Her eyes landed on the window.

"It's locked. Don't bother."

Except it wasn't locked as it had been when I'd checked all the windows and doors earlier. The latch was broken. Knowing what her next move would be, I grabbed Ginny's gun, which I'd stashed beneath my shirt, and aimed it at her. Her arms shot up, and she said, "Sheesh, you don't need to pull a gun on me, Sloane. I'm not sure what's gotten into you tonight, but I'm not the bad guy here."

Except she *was* the bad guy, and I intended to prove it.

She took a deep breath, and shadows of sadness crossed her expression.

Was it a ruse?

I couldn't tell.

Even if it was, I no longer cared.

"Ginny and I were on the brink. This close ..." She smooshed her index finger and her thumb together. "We were *this* close to, uh, breaking open a bad thing."

I leaned against the doorjamb, determined to keep her talking. "You don't say."

She moved around the desk and stood next to it. "Right. Yeah, so we were going to take the notebooks to the police. We hoped to prove Diego was murdered."

"After Ginny died, why didn't you?" I asked. "And why is this the first time I'm hearing about it? Why didn't you tell us about the notebooks before?"

"I've been a wreck since Ginny passed away and afraid for my own life. If *I* knew about the notebooks, someone else must know about them too. That's why I waited until now."

I paused a moment, just long enough for her to breathe a long sigh of relief. She'd told her story and told herself I'd believed every word of it.

"I have to say, I'm disappointed," I said.

She cocked her head to the side, confused. "Disappointed? Why?"

"I thought you'd come up with a better story than that. I mean, it's not the worst I've ever heard, but it's far from the best."

I moved closer to her. She was now leaning against the side of the desk, and I was giving her no space, my anger on the rise with every stupid lie she told.

"Here's what I think, Tara Simmons," I said. "I think you're no friend of this family. I think you're a con artist. You're involved in a plot to kill innocent people and benefiting from those 'accidental' deaths. Blood money, which you covet. I want the *real* story, and this is your last chance to give it to me. What happened to Diego and Ginny Alvarez?"

She hesitated and I prepared myself for another round of lies, and then she snapped, shrieking, "You want the truth? Fine! I hated them both with their perfect love, and their perfect life, and their perfect family!"

I jerked back in shock, and just as I did so, she dropped down and shot past me toward the door.

The little snake.

I wasn't letting this woman out of my sight. She may have been fast, but I was faster. She managed to make it to the hallway before I leapt toward her with a nice clean chop to the back of her neck.

She fell facedown—like the lump of garbage she was—and moaned.

I reached for the gun, which I'd dropped in the process, and straddled her, holding her in place.

"Sloane, what is—" I looked over my shoulder to see Maddie with cell phone in hand, staring at the spectacular scene. "Tara? What's going on? What are you doing—"

"Call 911, Maddie," I shouted. "Now."

Maddie snapped out of her stupor and dialed.

Tara wiggled around, trying to free herself from my grip, but I held firm.

"Let go of me!" she screamed.

Not a chance.

The 911 operator answered, and Maddie shouted, "There's been a break in at ..." and she gave the house number.

The cops were on their way.

Tara was going to jail.

Just when the surprises seemed to be over for the evening, Louie poked his head around the corner, and for the first time, I heard him speak.

41

"You killed my mom!" Louie shouted.

He was shaking, his face red and tear-stained, and he was pointing at Tara's hand.

Maddie grabbed him, swooping him into her arms. She looked at Tara's hand, and then at Louie. "What are you trying to tell us, honey?"

"That ... her ring. I saw it!"

"What did you see?"

"It was on the gun."

He inhaled a shuddering breath and then set free all of the pent-up rage he'd been holding inside of him. "I saw it on the gun and then the gun went off and my mom fell down, and I knew she was dead, and I ran and ran, and then a guy came after me, and I thought he was gonna kill me too."

He collapsed against Maddie, who pulled him in tight and stroked his hair.

And there it was in its entirety.

We had our killer.

"Take him out of here," I said.

"You sure?" Maddie said. "You got her?"

"Oh yeah. She's not going anywhere."

Maddie took Louie to his room, and I grabbed hold of Tara, shoving her against the wall. "Don't move a freaking muscle. Understand?"

"Or what? What are you going to do to me, Sloane? I bet you've never even fired a weapon before."

"You and I ... we don't know each other well. You have no idea what I'm capable of, and believe me when I say, you don't *want* to know. But hey, if you feel like taking your chances, make a move. It's been a few months since I've had any target practice."

Tara fought me for a minute and then lost steam and slumped over, holding her head in her hands. Down the hall I could hear Louie's muffled sobs from beyond the door, and it took everything in me not to slap Tara across the face. She deserved the same fate she'd bestowed on Ginny—a bullet to the head followed by her body being weighted down and dumped in the river.

I shifted my attention to the silver ring on her hand. It was large and garish, shaped like a woman's face, with diamonds for the eyes and snakes for the hair. No wonder Louie had recognized it.

In Greek mythology, Medusa represented a female full of power, a jealous woman, whose hair symbolized death and rebirth.

How fitting.

The sound of talking and shouting and police radios could be heard outside, and then someone pounded on the front door. Maddie rushed to open it. The police officer assigned to keep an eye on things rushed in, a look of relief on his face when he realized I'd disabled our uninvited guest. A few minutes later, Detective Flint came through the door, gun drawn, followed by Kat Smart, who'd already whipped out a pair of cuffs.

Flint said, "Tara Simmons, we've had our eye on you and your whole insurance racket ever since the death of Diego Alvarez."

I stared at him in disbelief. "You've *known* how dangerous she was, and you didn't—" I stepped toward him with fists clenched, even though I had no intention of using them.

Smart stepped forward and placed a hand on my shoulder. "We didn't know for sure until now. Plus, you, eh … well, Flint said you were the type of woman who could take care of herself. Judging by the gun in your hand, I'd say he's right. I'm going to need you to put it down."

I did as she asked.

"We'll explain everything later," Smart said. "Let's get this murderer out of this house first."

Tara kept her head down as they led her to a squad car. From the couch, Louie glared at her, while Maddie sneered at her in disgust. Out the door and down the front steps she went. Neighbors everywhere, gawking, whispering, pointing.

Smart led her to the back of the squad car and pushed down on Tara's head so Tara wouldn't bump it by getting in … but *somehow*, she bumped it anyway and howled in pain.

Smart turned around to face me, a grin on her face.

Thatta girl!

42

Flint and Smart returned the next day to brief us. They thanked us for our help, which was something I wasn't used to hearing from law enforcement given my line of work. They also offered a special thank-you to Louie, who was awarded a policeman's hat with the TSPD logo on it for the bravery he'd shown. It was kids-sized and looked adorable atop his thick curls.

As it turned out, Tara Simmons was the brain behind the madness and had found willing participants in a few muscles and slimeballs around town to assist in her felonious activities—insurance fraud and murder. Leo was one of the slimeballs, of course, and would be dealing with sentencing of some sort. Same for Frank the Skinny Thug too. Sure enough, the tattooed man at the boat had drugged Nick's beer. Nick, it seemed, was unaware of his wife's dealings.

As for Dom, he appeared to be innocent too.

The Tarpon Springs PD admitted they'd begun to suspect something was awry when Diego died, sensing a pattern of frequent 'accidental deaths,' but they couldn't find irrefutable evidence to prove the deaths weren't accidental. None of the insurance companies doubted the stories and had all paid up on the policies. Through threats to the surviving wives—a few of whom confessed to the police that they'd participated in covering up their husband's murders—the benefits were then shared with the criminals who were involved.

When the money started rolling in, Tara's greed got the better of her. She knew Ginny was closing in, having picked up where she'd left off with her husband Diego and their research into the possibility of a scam—killing off husbands for the insurance money. The one thing Ginny hadn't realized was her closest friend was the warlord she'd been pursuing all along. In her naivety, she had confided in Tara, a mistake that ended her life. Tara had shot Ginny in cold blood and had her thugs hide the body, tossing it in the river.

When those involved were arrested and interrogated, Detectives Flint and Smart offered a plea deal to one person—whichever thug came forward first to spill every last detail about Tara's illegal enterprise. Frank stepped right up, admitting Diego's death had not been ordered by Tara. At some point, the nefarious group became aware Diego was investigating the accidental murders. Tara suggested they watch him for a time to see how far he'd go with his suspicions. The suggestion didn't bode well with the tattooed man. Against Tara's wishes, he orchestrated Diego's unfortunate death himself.

And what about Nick's accident?

Once the murders began, Tara started a torrid love affair with the tattooed man. For a time, she considered divorcing Nick, deciding his lifestyle was far too vanilla for her liking. The tattooed man had a better idea, one Tara didn't go along with at first. But as the murders continued, and the old Tara was stripped away and replaced with a new, much more corrupt version, greed got the better of her. The idea of taking out a life insurance policy on Nick was too hard to resist. Once in place, all they needed to do was to wait for the right time to enact their plan to end Nick's life. A day at the beach provided it.

Given everything that had happened, Maddie was holding up

well, thankful the mystery of her sister's murder had been resolved before the funeral, which was slated for Saturday, three days from now. Her large family, scattered across the world, would soon all be together—or most of them, anyway—to honor Ginny Alvarez and send her home. No doubt Ginny would have been proud knowing her and Diego's research had not been for naught. And that their son had done his part in the catching of a killer.

Maddie and I sat in low-slung beach chairs on the side of the causeway at Howard Park, watching Louie—wearing his *bravery* hat, as he called it—and Charlie run around in the sand and water. Louie was skilled at throwing a frisbee. He'd sling it out over the water, and Charlie would retrieve it and bring it back.

I watched him for a time and then turned toward Maddie. "How are you feeling today?"

"Numb. But at least we know what happened now. Thank you, Sloane."

"I know we planned to continue our vacation for the next several weeks, but I'd understand if you'd rather go home. It's a lot to process. You need time to heal."

"If I go home, I'll just stew over it, which isn't like me. I say we keep going. Being with you is all the healing I need."

I smiled at her and said, "So, when does your sister Christine get here?"

"Friday. I talked to Louie this morning. He seems happy about going to live with her, and she just adores him. It will be good for them both. She'll give him a great life."

A great life.

It was all I'd hoped for him.

And soon, he'd have it.

43

The viewing had just taken place, and we were heading over to the cemetery to complete the funeral process. Somehow, Leo had been released on bail and decided it was a good idea to slip over to the funeral before anyone could stop him. Christine was none too pleased.

"What the hell were you thinking, Leo? Huh?" She swatted at him with her wide black hat. "You are such scum."

Leo held his arms around his head, trying to escape her wrath. "I just got in over my head. I helped the police though. I did. I didn't know Tara was going to shoot Ginny. I just thought she was going to threaten her. I swear."

It didn't matter what he said. She just kept coming at him. "If it wasn't for you ..." Swat, swat, swat. "You will burn in hell for your role in my sister's murder! Burn in hell!"

Swat, swat, swat.

Everyone watched.

No one stopped her.

It was years in the making, but now Leo was receiving his just due, not only from the sentence he might receive as a participant in

Tara's scam, but also from Christine. She'd become a strong woman now and had no fear of her abusive ex-husband, Leo Fratnik. Those days were long gone.

As family and friends headed to Ginny's final resting place, I broke from the group and made a beeline for Leo. I stood in front of him, blocking him from moving any closer to Ginny's gravesite.

"Where do you think *you're* going?" I asked. "You don't belong here. Leave before I make an even bigger scene than your ex-wife just did."

He snickered and tried to get by me.

I shoved him, forcing him back. "Last warning. Get out of here."

I felt a hand slide into mine, and I looked down. Louie smiled up at me. Then he gave Leo the meanest face he could muster, and said, "Go away. I don't like you! Nobody likes you!"

It was the reprimand of all reprimands.

Without a word, Leo turned and skulked away.

Satisfied, Louie headed toward Christine. Maddie was seated with her family at the front, and I hung back on the sidelines. This was a time for family—her family.

Maddie turned, searching for me. Our eyes locked, and she waved me toward her. I "pardoned" my way through the crowd and leaned down. "Hey," I said. "Are you okay?"

She patted the empty seat next to her. "What are you doing hiding back there? You're family. Sit your butt down."

It was Maddie's way of saying *I love you.*

I sat, and she leaned her head on my shoulder.

Christine held Louie close, and the preacher began his message. He spoke of Ginny's early life, what she was like as a child, and about the doting wife and mother she'd been in the years before her death. There was laughter. There were tears. And then there was Louie who walked his single red rose up to the hole in the earth and dropped it in. And even though his voice was tiny in comparison to the vastness of the space, his words echoed throughout the crowd, words no one would ever forget.

"I'll love you forever, Momma."

44

Another Monday had rolled around, a week since Ginny's body had been discovered. It seemed like an eternity ago *and* just yesterday all at the same time.

Christine would be staying at the Alvarez home for an undetermined length of time, to avoid further disruption of Louie's life. Maddie and I had moved back to the comfort of Lynn's inn. We sat across from each other at the massive table in the inn's dining room. The cherry pie was going down easy, as was the champagne Lynn had insisted we share.

Before leaving us alone, she'd said, "I do believe now's the time to restart your vacation."

She was right.

After this trip was over, I'd head back home to Cade, and we'd go on our own adventure. For the last several months, we'd been living in an Airbnb in New Orleans, and loving it. I had to admit, even though I hadn't been gone long, it seemed like a lot longer than it had been. I'd missed him.

"Where are we off to next?" I asked.

Maddie held up a finger, chugged what was left of her champagne, and pushed her glass in my direction. "Refill that for me. I'll be right back."

Off she went, and I could hear her feet pounding on the stairs as she headed toward our room.

I refilled both our glasses and ate the last bite of pie.

When she returned, her face was all mischief.

"Well?" I prompted. "Spill it."

She held up a small leather pouch. "Next, we're going to get our mojo on."

"Are we? And the little bag you're holding is ... what? Filled with fairy dust to get us there?"

She smiled. "Great guess. Try again."

"What does this bag have to do with our next stop? Where are we going? You can't keep me—"

"Savannah, Georgia!" She waved the bag. "This is a mojo bag, a medicine bag, a hoodoo thing."

She had my attention. "And Savannah has these things?" A vague thought crossed my mind, remembering a popular book I'd read about Savannah. I snapped my fingers. "Savannah's where ... that book ..."

She nodded. "It's called 'The Book' in Savannah, girlfriend. *Midnight in the Garden of Good and Evil.*"

"That's the one. There was some sort of hoodoo or voodoo or root doctor involved, right?"

She waved a hand at me. "That was just part of it." She slid the bag across the table.

I picked it up and played with it for a few seconds, loving the feel of the buckskin in my hand. Then I pulled open the drawstring and took a look. Empty. "Isn't there supposed to be bones or something inside here?"

"You think I'm going to mess around with that? I have no idea what I'm doing. It was just to get you fired up about the trip."

"And you have succeeded."

She leaned across the table and whispered, "It's a town filled with mystery and history. And the odd ghost ... or fifty."

I quirked an eyebrow. "Sounds like it's right up our alley."

...

Thank you for reading The Silent Boy, the first book in the Sloane & Maddie, Peril Awaits spinoff series.

We hope you enjoyed getting to know the characters in this story as much as we enjoyed writing them for you. This is a continuing series with more books coming after the one you just read.

You can find the series order (as of the date of this printing) in the "Books by Cheryl Bradshaw" section below.

Book two in the series, The Moonlight Child, will be on pre-order shortly. We can't wait for you to read it!

Enjoy The Silent Boy?

You can show your appreciation by leaving a review on Amazon, Barnes & Noble, Apple Books, Google Play, Kobo, or Goodreads.

If you write a review, please be sure to email Cheryl at cheryl@authorcherylbradshaw.com so she can express her gratitude. She does her best to reply to as many emails as she can, and she appreciates every piece of mail she receives.

About Cheryl Bradshaw

Cheryl Bradshaw is a *New York Times* and 11-time *USA Today* best-selling author writing in the genres of mystery, thriller, paranormal suspense, and romantic suspense, among others. Her novel *Stranger in Town* (Sloane Monroe series #4) was a Shamus Award finalist for Best PI Novel of the Year, and her novel *I Have a Secret* (Sloane Monroe series #3) was an eFestival of Words winner for Best Thriller.

Raised in California, most of the year she can be found exploring the tropics in Cairns, Australia, where she currently lives, or traveling the world.

About Janet Fix

She's an editor, and yes, her last name really is Fix.

A freelance editor and writer, Janet Fix offers decades of experience in the words services industry, including all levels of editing and ghostwriting in a variety of genres. As owner of thewordverve inc., she acts as a book shepherd of sorts, guiding writers through their publishing journeys with a heavy focus on quality editing.

She is author of a children's book series called Ranch Hero, and now has truly come out from behind the red pen to coauthor her first novel alongside bestselling author Cheryl Bradshaw. The Silent Boy is the first in a spin-off series based on Cheryl's Sloane Monroe Mysteries.

A graduate of the University of South Florida, Tampa, with a degree in speech communication, she currently lives in the North Georgia mountains, where creative inspiration abounds.

...

All published books are heavily researched, proofed, and edited.

Should you find any issues in the book you just read, please forward them to her assistant at cherylbradshawbooks@hotmail.com so they can be sent along to the publisher.

Never Miss One of Cheryl's Book's Again!

Sign up for Cheryl Bradshaw's "Killer Newsletter" today to be the first to know when a new book is released and to enter to win fun bookish swag. You'll also receive a free eBook just for joining! Learn more here: cherylbradshaw.com/get-a-free-ebook/

BOOKS BY CHERYL BRADSHAW

Sloane Monroe Series

Silent as the Grave (Prequel, Book 0)

When the body of Rebecca Barlow is found floating in the lake, private investigator Sloane Monroe takes on her very first homicide.

Black Diamond Death (Book 1)

Charlotte Halliwell has a secret. But before revealing it to her sister, she's found dead.

Murder in Mind (Book 2)

A woman is found murdered, the serial killer's trademark "S" carved into her wrist.

I Have a Secret (Book 3)

Doug Ward has been running from his past for twenty years. But after his fourth whisky of the night, he doesn't want to keep quiet, not anymore.

Stranger in Town (Book 4)

A frantic mother runs down the aisles, searching for her missing daughter. But little Olivia is already gone.

Bed of Bones (Book 5) (USA Today Bestselling Book)

Sometimes even the deepest, darkest secrets find their way to the surface.

Flirting with Danger (Book 5.5) A Sloane Monroe Short Story

A fancy hotel. A weekend getaway. For Sloane Monroe, rest has finally arrived, until the lights go out, a woman screams, and Sloane's nightmare begins.

Hush Now Baby (Book 6) (USA Today Bestselling Book)

Serena Westwood tiptoes to her baby's crib and looks inside, startled to find her newborn son is gone.

Dead of Night (Book 6.5) A Sloane Monroe Short Story

After her mother-in-law is fatally stabbed, Wren is seen fleeing with the bloody knife. Is Wren the killer, or is a dark, scandalous family secret to blame?

Gone Daddy Gone (Book 7) (USA Today Bestselling Book)

A man lurks behind Shelby in the park. Who is he? And why does he have a gun?

Smoke & Mirrors (Book 8) (USA Today Bestselling Book)

Grace Ashby wakes to the sound of a horrifying scream. She races down the hallway, finding her mother's lifeless body on the floor in a pool of blood. Her mother's boyfriend Hugh is hunched over her, but is Hugh really her mother's killer?

Sloane Monroe Stories: Deadly Sins

Deadly Sins: Sloth (Book 1)

Darryl has been shot, and a mysterious woman is sprawled out on the floor in his hallway. She's dead too. Who is she? And why have they both been murdered?

Deadly Sins: Wrath (Book 2)

Headlights flash through Maddie's car's back windshield, someone following close behind. When her car careens into a nearby tree, the chase comes to an end. But for Maddie, the end is just the beginning.

Deadly Sins: Lust (Book 3)

Marissa Calhoun sits alone on a beach-like swimming hole nestled on Australia's foreshore. Tonight, the lagoon is hers and hers alone. Or is it?

Deadly Sins: Greed (Book 4)

It was just another day for mob boss Giovanni Luciana until he took his car for a drive.

Deadly Sins: Envy (Book 5)

A cryptic message. A missing niece. And only twenty-four hours to pay.

Sloane & Maddie, Peril Awaits (Co-Authored with Janet Fix)

The Silent Boy (Book 1)

In the hallway of a local tavern, six-year-old Louie Alvarez waits for his mother to take him home. A scream rips through the air, followed by the sound of a gun being fired. Louie freezes, then turns, with a single thought on his mind: RUN.

Georgiana Germaine Series

Little Girl Lost (Book 1)

For the past two years, former detective Georgiana "Gigi" Germaine has been living off the grid, until today, when she hears some disturbing news that shakes her.

Little Lost Secrets (Book 2)

When bones are discovered inside the walls during a home renovation, Georgiana uncovers a secret that's linked to her father's untimely death thirty years earlier.

Little Broken Things (Book 3)

Twenty-year-old Olivia Spencer sits at her desk in her mother's bookshop, dreaming about her upcoming wedding. The store may be closed, but she's not alone, and her dream is about to become her worst nightmare.

Addison Lockhart Series

Grayson Manor Haunting (Book 1)

When Addison Lockhart inherits Grayson Manor after her mother's untimely death, she unlocks a secret that's been kept hidden for over fifty years.

Rosecliff Manor Haunting (Book 2)

Addison Lockhart jolts awake. The dream had seemed so real. Eleven-year-old twins Vivian and Grace were so full of life, but they couldn't be. They've been dead for over forty years.

Blackthorn Manor Haunting (Book 3)

Addison Lockhart leans over the manor's window, gasping when she feels a hand on her back. She grabs the windowsill to brace herself, but it's too late--she's already falling.

Belle Manor Haunting (Book 4)

A vehicle barrels through the stop sign, slamming into the car Addison Lockhart is inside before fleeing the scene. Who is the driver of the other car? And what secrets within the walls of Belle Manor will provide the answer?

Till Death do us Part Novella Series

Whispers of Murder (Book 1)

It was Isabelle Donnelly's wedding day, a moment in time that should have been the happiest in her life...until it ended in murder.

Echoes of Murder (Book 2)

When two women are found dead at the same wedding, medical examiner Reagan Davenport will stop at nothing to discover the identity of the killer.

Stand-Alone Novels

Eye for Revenge (USA Today Bestselling Book)

Quinn Montgomery wakes to find herself in the hospital. Her childhood best friend Evie is dead, and Evie's four-year-old son witnessed it all. Traumatized over what he saw, he hasn't spoken.

The Perfect Lie

When true-crime writer Alexandria Weston is found murdered on the last stop of her book tour, fellow writer Joss Jax steps in to investigate.

Hickory Dickory Dead (USA Today Bestselling Book)

Maisie Fezziwig wakes to a harrowing scream outside. Curious, she walks outside to investigate, and Maisie stumbles on a grisly murder that will change her life forever.

Roadkill (USA Today Bestselling Book)

Suburban housewife Juliette Granger has been living a secret life ... a life that's about to turn deadly for everyone she loves.

www.ingramcontent.com/pod-product-compliance
Ingram Content Group UK Ltd.
Pitfield, Milton Keynes, MK11 3LW, UK
UKHW021937190726
13853UKWH00004B/1506

9 798536 508343